Brat

Brat

A Novel

GABRIEL SMITH

PENGUIN PRESS

NEW YORK

2024

PENGUIN PRESS
An imprint of Penguin Random House LLC
penguinrandomhouse.com

LIBRARY OF CONGRESS CATALOGING-IN-PUBLICATION DATA

Names: Smith, Gabriel, author.
Title: Brat : a novel / Gabriel Smith.
Description: New York : Penguin Press, 2024.
Identifiers: LCCN 2023056718 (print) | LCCN 2023056719 (ebook) |
    ISBN 9780593656877 (hardcover) | ISBN 9780593656884 (ebook)
Subjects: LCGFT: Paranormal fiction. | Humorous fiction. | Novels.
Classification: LCC PR6119.M5748 B73 2024 (print) |
    LCC PR6119.M5748 (ebook) | DDC 823/.92—dc23/eng/20231208
LC record available at https://lccn.loc.gov/2023056718
LC ebook record available at https://lccn.loc.gov/2023056719

Printed in the United States of America
1st Printing

Designed by Amanda Dewey

For Gian

Brat

I was in the waiting room. Then I was in the examination room. There was a chair, and another chair, and a hydraulic doctor bed. Sit down, the doctor said. I didn't know where. Not on the bed, he said. I sat on a chair.

"I think I have a concussion," I said.

"Why do you think that?" the doctor said.

"My nephew hit me."

"He hit you?"

"In the nose. Then in the back of the head."

"How old is he?" the doctor said.

"Fourteen," I said.

"Okay," he said, "take off your shirt."

"Really?" I said.

"Sure," the doctor said. I unbuttoned my shirt.

He shone a light in my eyes.

The light was on the end of a cone. The cone was set at ninety degrees on the end of a metal rod. It looked like a thing dentists use for looking at mouths.

"No concussion," the doctor said. It didn't seem like he could tell that just by shining a cone in my eyes.

"Looks like you have a little eczema here, though," he said. He pointed to my chest then spun away in his chair.

I looked down at myself. There was a red patch, and what

looked like a slightly raised piece of dead skin in the center of my chest. Just to the right of where I assumed my heart was.

"Okay," I said.

"Don't worry," he said, looking at his computer, "very treatable. I'm writing you a prescription. For hydrocortisol cream."

"Don't you mean hydrocortisone?"

"Yes," he said, "hydrocortisone. That is what I said."

My brother's wife, when I was back at the house, said I shouldn't have provoked him.

"He's very sensitive," she said.

"What?" I said. "I didn't provoke him."

"He loved your dad," my brother's wife said. "They had a real connection."

"I don't see what that has to do with anything."

"Are you really going to wear that outfit?" she said. I was wearing a T-shirt with lots of Phils on it: Phil Leotardo, Phil Neville, the Philippines, the concept of "Philanthropy," Philadelphia (the spread), the London Philharmonic, Prince Philip.

"What?" I said. "No. I am going to wear a suit."

"It has a stain on it. You can't wear that."

"I am going to change," I said.

My brother walked into the kitchen and kissed his wife on the forehead as she walked out of it. He started doing something in a cupboard.

"You should wear the Phil T-shirt to Dad's funeral," he said.

"I am going to change," I said, and left the room.

I looked at myself in the half-steamed bathroom mirror. This was the house I grew up in.

The doctor was right about the skin on my chest, just to the right of where I assumed my heart was. It looked all weird.

I picked at the skin. It came away painlessly.

Just a little at first. It made a thick and translucent white flap. I flicked at it with my fingernail. I pulled at it. More pulled away like damp paper. Over my left nipple, then right up to my armpit.

It started to sting a little like it was meant to stay on. I stopped tearing myself. The skin just hung there.

Then I kept going.

I couldn't walk around with half my chest hanging off me.

Once I'd torn it mostly off, I had an alarmingly large piece of skin in my hands. I looked at it.

It was me but losing its shape, still slightly ridged where it had run over my rib cage.

I looked at my body in the mirror.

There was a long rift where I'd removed the dead skin. It poked outward, up the side of me, almost imperceptibly, like the unfindable edge of a Sellotape roll.

I didn't know what to do with the skin that had come off. I couldn't leave it in the bathroom bin where my brother or his wife would find it. And I didn't want to flush it, either.

I thought about putting it in my pocket and taking it downstairs and wrapping it in a plastic bag and disposing of it secretly. But that felt insane. And I didn't want to get caught doing it.

I dropped the skin into the bathtub. It made a slap sound.

I turned the showerhead on all the way. I pointed it at the skin. After a moment it began to break apart, as if decomposing, and the tiny pieces of it were carried by the spiraling water down the sloping porcelain, down into the plughole.

After the funeral, at the wake, which was at the house, my nephew apologized for punching me.

"I'm sorry for punching you in your head," he said.

"No problem," I said.

"I just get so angry sometimes," he said.

"Right," I said.

"Don't you?" he said.

I poured myself more wine from the bottle I was guarding from everyone else. The new skin was tender under my shirt, under my jacket.

The living room was large but full of mourners. My uncle by marriage was holding court on refreshments.

"Yes, I borrowed it from work," he said. "From the work canteen."

He was talking about a large metal urn that stored and dispensed near-boiling water.

"I thought a lot of people would want tea," my uncle said, "and that this would make it easier."

"It must have been hard to get here," I said, "with all the hot water in."

"What?" he said.

"Imagine if it spilled on someone," I said. "They'd get all burned."

"No," he said, "you don't transport it full. That'd be dangerous."

"That's what I'm saying," I said.

"What are you doing for work at the moment?" he said. "Still writing? Like your parents?"

"Yeah," I said.

"And the money's all right? I read an article about how books don't make money anymore. Barely any of you make any money."

My brother walked over. He was holding a glass of wine and a beer.

"I see you have two drinks," I said, to him. "Nice."

He tried to hand the beer to my uncle, who put his palms up and made a goofy face, then mimed driving a car.

"Thanks for apologizing to your nephew," my brother said, to me.

"I didn't," I said.

"He really appreciated it."

"I didn't apologize. He apologized to me."

"Sure," my brother said.

"Hey," I said. "Some of my skin came off earlier."

My brother was a plastic surgeon. That was his job.

"What?" he said.

"In the shower. Like a reptile."

"Your skin came off?"

"Like a reptile," I repeated.

"That sounds like eczema. You should see a doctor."

"You are a doctor."

"I'm not a skin doctor."

"You are a skin doctor."

"No, I'm not. I'm a surgeon. I'm not looking at your eczema skin."

"I saw a doctor today," I said, "and he gave me a cream." I tried to pour myself more wine from my bottle but it was empty.

"So use the cream," my brother said.

I walked away to get another drink.

Back in the kitchen, a neighbor from down the road said it had been a beautiful ceremony.

"That was a beautiful ceremony," she said.

She was older than sixty and wore purple all the time. Even to funerals.

"It was?" I said. But she thought I was just agreeing.

"He would have loved it."

"He would have?"

"He would have found it very moving."

"I thought he might have found it disappointing," I said, "being dead."

"Yes, he would have found it very moving," she said. "He was a very emotional man. A true artist."

I thought about my father in the audience of my brother's school flute recital, holding a biro and the photocopied program, ticking off each act as it finished.

I thought about my father in the audience of my brother's school prize-giving, slumped. I thought about him sitting up, suddenly, when a small girl, maybe nine, won an award for "dance." I thought about him saying loudly, incredulously—loud enough for parents to shush him—"Darts?"

"You knew him pretty well," I said.

"We had a connection," she said. "He was a true artist."

I looked around for a different conversation.

"And so kind," she said, "staying with your mother. After everything."

I drank the last of my new glass of wine. I put the glass down on the counter hard.

"Listen, you stupid purple bitch," I said. "Shut the fuck up about my dad."

I woke up hungover in my childhood bedroom. I was still wearing my shoes and trousers.

My white shirt had quite a lot of blood on it. My head hurt under my face.

I took my shoes off and went downstairs to make coffee. My brother's wife was in the kitchen already.

"Coffee?" I said. I gestured at her with a mug. She didn't say anything. She just made a sound and left the room.

My brother walked in as she walked out. He kissed her on the forehead as they passed each other.

"Got some blood on you," he said. "Make me some coffee."

I sat down at the breakfast island in the middle of the kitchen. The tea urn was gone. But there were glasses and mugs everywhere. The foily remains of wake snacks.

I took my cigarettes out and lit one.

"Jesus Christ," my brother said.

"My head hurts," I said.

"She got you good," he said.

"I should have hit her back," I said.

"As if you could," he said. "She made you look like a little bitch."

"Yeah," I said.

"You are a little bitch," my brother's wife shouted, from another room.

I heard my brother and his wife leave to get some air or something. So I called my girlfriend.

It rang once. Then the line went dead. There was no option for voicemail.

I let myself count the days in my head. I had last seen her three weeks ago tomorrow.

Maybe she had blocked my number now.

The wood felt cold and crumb-covered against my forehead.

My brother drove me and his wife to our mother's nursing home. My brother's wife made sure she sat up front so I sat in the back of their car, which was small, but new, and expensive-seeming.

"How was the funeral?" my mother said, from her chair, which was disgusting.

"It was beautiful," my brother's wife said. "It was a really beautiful ceremony, Rebecca. Everyone said so."

"I'm so glad," my mother said.

"Have you got everything you need, Mum? Do you need us to bring anything?" my brother said, louder than necessary. My mother ignored him.

"What happened to your face?" she said.

"Cheryl hit me," I said.

"Why would she do that?" my mother said.

"I was defending Dad's honor."

"He called her a stupid purple bitch," my brother said.

"Shut up," I said.

"Oh, no," my mother said.

"I didn't," I said.

"Oh, no," my mother said.

"And my skin is peeling off, Mum," I said. "I'm very frightened."

"What?" my mother said.

"Nothing," my brother said. "He is just joking. He has some eczema. He is just joking."

"I hope you didn't hit her back," my mother said.

"I got her good. Spark out," I said. I mimed a jab with my right. "Cheryl's in the hospital."

"Oh, no," my mother said.

"No, he didn't," my brother's wife said. "He's just trying to upset you. He didn't hit her."

"She's messed up," I said. "She'll never look the same."

"Oh, no," my mother said.

Maybe we should just kill Mum," I said, in the foyer of the nursing home, as we were leaving. "No parents, no rules. Clean break."

"Shut up," my brother's wife said.

"What did you say the advance on your book was?" my brother said.

He meant my second book, the book I had told everyone I was writing, and got paid an advance on.

I had told everyone it was about an elderly gardener. The gardener lives near Chernobyl, in Soviet times.

The gardener dies because he's so old. In the middle of the gardener's funeral rites, the nearby power plant explodes. The funeral is abandoned halfway through.

The gardener becomes a *dybbuk*, which was a kind of Jewish ghost I'd seen in a movie. He has to wander around the Earth endlessly, gardening or something, until something gets sorted out.

That was as far as I'd gotten. I hadn't actually written any of it yet.

I had tried. But every time I tried I just didn't.

"Fifty five thou," I said. "Clean, nonsequential bills."

"Fucking hell," my brother said.

"That's wonderful news," my brother's wife said, "congratulations. You won't need to be in London. You can help get the house in order. For the sale."

"Yes, good idea," I said, thinking about not having to pay rent anymore.

It was autumn and there were leaves everywhere. I decided to go back to London to get things. On the train I sat facing the wrong direction and looked out the window. The air was full of rain. I was carried backward into it.

In my flat the furniture was still there. The sofa, the television, the stereo, the gifted soft-furnishings.

But when I opened the wardrobe to get a clean jumper it was empty. Or, two-thirds empty. All my girlfriend's things had disappeared. Her dresses, blouses, skirts. Her floating light-fabricked trousers. Her multiple heavy winter coats. I went to the dresser and checked the drawers that belonged to her.

But they were empty, too. All that was left was lint, and the decrepit sprigs of lavender she believed would ward off moths.

Then I noticed the bookshelves. They were also mainly empty. So was the bathroom. All the stupid and expensive houseplants had disappeared.

I was surprised at how few of the things we owned together belonged to me. There were outlines of dust all around the places her things used to live.

The air smelled different somehow.

I looked around for a note or something. But there wasn't

one. So I tried calling her phone again and it rang once and then went silent.

I went out onto the balcony for a while.

The sun was setting gray.

When I woke, it felt like someone was watching me.

I sat up in bed for a second. Then I turned on the lights. But there was nobody in the room. And the curtains were closed.

I noticed that in my sleep I'd built a person out of pillows next to me. Maybe so it felt as if she was still in the bed.

I could feel my heart pushing my chest.

When I couldn't get back to sleep I dressed and had a drink. My girlfriend had taken some of the wine but left the spirits. After that I felt a bit better.

I started packing possessions into the suitcase she hadn't taken. It was the ugliest one. We had named it "Ugly Green."

By the time dawn was done I was ready to leave. I wrote an email on my phone to the estate agent saying we were vacating the flat; that they could dispose of the remaining contents, at our expense, as they saw fit.

Then I tried calling her again. But it rang out.

I rolled Ugly Green to the door. I turned around and began to wipe the dust outlines of her possessions from the shelves and counters and other furniture surfaces. But then I decided I did not feel like it. So I gave up.

The train back to the house was half-filled with commuters, in various states of rained-on, all umbrellas and ugly laptops. They thinned out as we got farther out of the city, until I was alone, in the train carriage, in the countryside.

From the outside, once I was back at it, the house looked very empty.

The plants around it seemed to have gotten bigger.

There were vines growing up one of the walls. They were almost touching the glass of a ground floor window.

My key was loud in the door. Nobody shouted hello.

In the bathroom, I picked at the skin on my hand. It felt dry and funny.

The skin pulled upward, from my wrist, all the way from my palms and fingers, and then across the back of my hand.

I just kept pulling, until it had come away from all my fingers and shifting hand veins. The skin came away in a single piece. It didn't hurt. I looked at it. It looked like a glove of myself.

I threw the skin into the bathtub. I turned the showerhead on and aimed at the skin and watched as it disintegrated and was carried down the drain.

My brother and his wife were back in their big and increasingly valuable house in London. So I was alone in this one.

It was mid-afternoon. I got drunk. Then I went to bed and slept dreamlessly.

It was almost afternoon again. I was not sure how I had slept so long.

I wrote a message to my brother and his wife to confirm that I would be living in the house, ostensibly to help clear it out for the sale.

I did not want to do that. But saying it would make them feel okay with me living in the house.

After I wrote that message I looked at Twitter. My girlfriend had a new story out. In *Guernica*. She still had me blocked. But the story was all over everyone else's Twitters. So I saw it anyway. Everyone was calling the story excellent, dark, funny, astute, etc.

I opened my laptop to look at it on there. I scrolled all the way to the bottom.

I didn't recognize her new author photo. Her hair was shorter than it was. Beside the photo it said: *Kei Kagirinaku is a writer from London.*

Downstairs, I heard the television say: *the magnetic North Pole is moving increasingly toward Siberia, away from Canada.* I didn't remember turning it on.

Again I had the feeling someone was watching me. So I stood up and closed the bedroom door. But I couldn't shake the feeling. So I sat back down and started reading. The story was called "Cum Tributo."

CUM TRIBUTO

Volodislav Sukov, Russian oligarch, was mid-orgasm when the alarm at the National Gallery went off.

The alarm went off and a red light began to flash in the room he was in and then in the rooms adjacent and then the alarm made alarm noise, too.

Volodislav was alone. But then he wasn't. He was with the woman in the blue-black painting opposite him, now covered in his ejaculate, looking up, and to the left, and then, looking around, there were other faces too, painted.

And then the face of a female security attendant, eyes wide, face oscillating red and white. She looked frightened. But then she painted her face composed, and then she was stepping silently toward him, her hand heading to the two-way radio that hung on the side of her hip.

Volodislav Sukov was not just any oligarch. He was a top oligarch. He was the eighth richest and second most popular of all the oligarchs. Born in Saint Petersburg, Volodislav resided in Moscow on the top floors of a seventeen-story apartment complex. But he also lived in London, where he owned a Premier League football club. And he was regularly pictured on his superyacht, too.

He'd had four beautiful, long-term, non-overlapping girlfriends, and each girlfriend had in turn borne him a beautiful blond, blue-eyed child. Volodislav's four children were photographed regularly. They were photographed together at major sporting events, smiling. Or they were photographed posed in perfect lobbies, their father standing behind them. Or they were photographed leaving some hotel, headed, holding hands, toward some subtly armored car.

Volodislav made his money in oil, like all oligarchs. But he had diversified. He was in pharmaceuticals, and real estate, and infrastructure construction also. This was all carefully arranged. Nothing was in writing. But the appropriate kickbacks to the higher-ups—Putin—were kept in place. He felt safe from the Russians and from the Americans and from the British, too. Not that the British cared.

Like all oligarchs, Volodislav was a collector of art and other treasures.

And, like all oligarchs, Volodislav had a terrible, terrible secret.

The secret started when Volodislav was just a young oligarch. Thirty-odd.

Volodislav did not remember the girl. Volodislav did not remember the party, really.

But Volodislav did remember the room. The floor, half-covered in construction dust, the furniture all wrapped in taped-up transparent plastic.

Paintings leaned against the wall, unhung.

Volodislav remembered the paintings.

Volodislav remembered the paintings, and sneaking the girl out of the party. Half sneaking. Sneaking because it was fun. Not because anyone would stop him.

He snuck the girl in the stairwell. Then he snuck her upstairs, unclasped her.

"Not here," she said, in English.

So he snuck her into the unfinished room with the construction dust and the party below and the furniture wrapped in plastic and the paintings all on the floor, all leaned against walls.

He pushed her into the wall. She pushed back, but only with the middle of her. Didn't he know his lips were so dry?

Then she was satisfied that they'd gone far enough. So she knelt for him.

And when he came he came hard and quickly. She tried to catch it in her mouth but missed.

Volodislav had his eyes closed.

In his head he counted the soft snaps that happened in the middle of him.

Seven, eight, nine.

He slipped his shoulders in. He opened his eyes.

The girl was still there, knelt in front of him. But he had barely hit her, overshot. Some was in her mouth and on her chin and on her collarbone.

But most of him was behind her, and to the right. He had not landed on the dust floor or some plastic-covered furniture or the wall.

He had landed right on one of the paintings. A portrait. A pretty, young fat-faced woman dressed in blue, looking up and to the left into some yellow light. And Volodislav had shot himself all over her.

And Volodislav, right then, realized that it was the most beautiful thing he'd ever seen.

He looked at it and looked at it and looked at it.

The most beautiful thing he'd seen in his whole life.

He looked at it and looked at it and looked at it.

It was so beautiful.

He looked at it and looked at it and looked at it.

And he felt his insides collapse.

And when the girl returned with a previously concealed wet wipe and removed the drying ejaculate from the painted woman's face, Volodislav's heart broke forever.

All oligarchs are art collectors, but Volodislav began to buy in earnest. He became obsessive. He studied the catalogs from Christie's and Sotheby's with religious and sexual fervor, purchasing everything he desired.

Volodislav loved the auctions, but due to the nature of his lifestyle could rarely attend them in person. Instead he sent representatives with instructions to outbid any other suitor. And Volodislav never lost.

Word grew about his collection. He bought a Caravaggio and two Botticellis, a young man by Peter Paul Rubens. A penitent Magdalene by Gerrit Dou. Works by Vermeer and Antiveduto Grammatica, Paolo Veronese. All portraits.

Rumors circulated. Not only had he started buying art in vast quantities, but instead of shipping the works to private climate-controlled storage facilities in tax havens (like other sensible investors), Volodislav was having the art handling companies bring the work to his homes in London, and Moscow, and even—inadvisably—to his superyacht, wherever it was moored. As a result he paid wildly over the odds for insurance services and taxation. People thought Volodislav Sukov was showing off his collection. It became fashionable to describe Volodislav Sukov as gaudy, uneducated, compulsive.

Volodislav did not care.

In private, Volodislav ejaculated onto each one. He loved the ceremony of it: the prior shower, the several white towels, the preparation of wet wipes and lighting and lubricant. The first time with each painted woman was always the very most perfect. Or close, but never quite.

Volodislav bought a very old and very, very beautiful wooden easel. He would place the painting on it and stand facing, stark naked, door locked. Volodislav instructed his staff that he was not to be disturbed.

After he came he wiped the cum away carefully.

People began to wonder why he never sold any of the paintings he purchased.

Only Volodislav knew.

When he was done with a painting, and the arrival of a new painting was imminent, he'd hang the used one in a room that he did not visit often in one of his residences that he did not visit often.

Then he would never look at it ever again.

Volodislav hated to look at them after.

Decades passed. Soon Volodislav bored of even the paintings he could afford. He needed more. He obsessively visited public galleries, making generous donations and learning everything there was to learn about their collections.

His reputation in the art world shifted. Though he was still thought of as tasteless and gaudy, Volodislav had donated so much money to galleries and other Art World institutions that he could be described as a philanthropist first, and collector second.

People forgot Volodislav was an oligarch. The Whitechapel Gallery opened a whole wing in the building next door, which he paid for. The Serpentine's summer season was subtitled with his surname, after the Sacklers were sent packing. Parties were hosted in his honor. And when debates were held over the influence of bad money on good culture, his name was never mentioned out of deference.

And this is how Volodislav Sukov came to be alone, after dark, in the National Gallery in London.

To be alone after dark in the National Gallery is a privilege—one afforded to friends of higher-level staff and generous benefactors. And Volodislav was now both. And, leaving his assigned assistant in the North Wing with some lesser Dutch work from the seventeenth century, he walked alone, heels clipping the cold and silent gallery floors.

And then he saw her.

In the Mond Room. *The Virgin in Prayer*, by Sassoferrato.

She was perfect.

Blue and pink and white like stained glass, or sweet wrappers, and full of her own light in the near-dark room.

Volodislav felt himself growing erect underneath his soft and expensive blue jeans. He touched himself through the fabric. He felt himself push back against his own touch.

He took a step closer to the painting.

Then another.

She was so perfect.

How had he never seen her before?

Volodislav could hear nothing but his heartbeat. He felt it pushing against his chest, the pulsing in his temples. He inched as far into the painting as the ankle-height wire barrier allowed. His toes crossed underneath it.

He unzipped his jeans and moved his penis out into the carefully conditioned air. He gripped it with his right hand and started masturbating himself. Slowly, at first, then faster.

He looked around for security cameras and saw them, watching him looking back at them, and for a moment the spell was broken.

But then he looked back at the painting and blood rushed back to him.

So he continued.

The orgasm came fast. It was uncontrollable and huge. Volodislav shot his ejaculate onto his hand, and onto the floor in front of him, and onto the painting itself. Great waves shook his body. He leaned back. The ejaculate covered the canvas. The frame, the foreground, and the face at the center of it.

And for that moment, everything was so perfect.

So perfect and beautiful.

And to avoid falling over backward Volodislav stepped forward, into the wire security barrier, and a red light began to flash in the room he was in, then in other rooms too, and then an alarm sound filled all of the rooms.

Volodislav looked around panicked. He was alone. But then he wasn't. There was the face in the painting, opposite him, now covered in his ejaculate, looking down, and then, looking around, there were other faces too, painted, and then the face of a female security attendant, eyes wide, face oscillating red and white, then painting her face composed, and stepping silently toward him, her hand heading to the two-way radio that hung on the side of her hip.

If anyone else had ejaculated onto a priceless work of art, they would have been arrested. But Volodislav was not anyone else. The incident was, in fact, never spoken of, and Volodislav died a few years later in a boating accident.

There were suspicions of foul play, but those in the know knew it was a simple accident.

These things happen.

People die in the strangest ways, once they're done living.

Volodislav's art collection was divided up between his differently mothered children.

Many galleries around the world still bear his name.

But even now, when art handlers go to move paintings in the Mond Room and shine their ultraviolet lights at the white walls to read the secret guidance written there in ultraviolet pen by past art handlers, they notice a strange stain on *The Virgin in Prayer*, invisible to the naked eye but still there, now, and probably for hundreds or thousands of years in the future.

The indelible ugliness of it.

The stain of something that was briefly perfect.

I looked again at the photo of my girlfriend. My body felt bad and full of movement.

I had not written anything in so long. This was a real story. She had never mentioned working on it.

And when I looked inside myself there were no finished stories. Just bad feelings, and movements I could make with my body, and in the middle of me all I could feel was a big black-blue constantly shifting geometric shape that had nothing inside. That was what was in the middle of me.

I thought about that for a bit. The bit inside me where there wasn't anything.

I did not feel like anyone was watching me then.

I noticed that I didn't feel like that because I just felt alone.

I lit a cigarette. I closed my laptop.

Then I opened it again and closed the tab so her face would not be there when I next opened my laptop.

Then I closed my laptop again.

I know I slept on the sofa that night because I woke up there. And because I came conscious two or three or four times, once the television had turned itself off and the room was dark. I had the feeling that there was someone in the room or at the window watching me sleep. But each time I would switch the dust-lined lamp on and see that I was alone in there and that all there was outside were windowpane-touching plants and quickly I would be pulled backward again, into my own eyelids.

I could hear the sound of something moving against the window. It was light now. At first I thought the sound was plant sound, vines knocking against glass. But as I became more awake it sounded more like animal sound. Or person sound.

The curtains were kind of open.

I turned my head on the sofa so I could see out of the window.

At first I saw nothing.

But then I saw some movement, at the corner of a curtain, outside the window. Something brown and tall.

Then it disappeared behind the curtain.

I stopped moving at all.

I kept watching the window for the brown tall thing.

I looked around the room for something I could hit someone with. I stood up but crouched.

I felt stupid. Like I was overreacting to nothing.

But I kept on creeping just the same.

It felt better to be prepared. And if it was a delivery man, or other visitor, I didn't want to have to talk to them right then. So it was better if they didn't see me.

I moved low to the window seat. But I still couldn't see anything out there.

I moved my head so I could see the edge of the front of the house. And there it was.

A person. The figure of one.

I only saw it for a moment. It was walking around the side of the house, down the overgrown path that went to the back garden.

I thought about how the back door of the house was not locked.

I went fast to the kitchen with its window onto the garden.

I thought about the person walking in the same direction as me, but outside the house.

I took a knife from the breakfast-bar knife block.

I listened for the sound of the back door opening. But it didn't.

I listened and waited.

Then I went over to the window.

I couldn't see anyone in the garden.

I looked very hard and for a very long time.

But I didn't see anything. Just the fucked-up garden shed's door swinging on its hinges in the wind at the bottom of the garden, and the also-moving shadows of the trees of the woods at the bottom of the garden on the overgrown grass, left there by morningish autumn light.

My parents' bedroom occupied the third floor of the house. The attic was there too, behind another door. Then behind that attic there was another attic, which was really the underneath roof of the house.

On my parents' dresser were around thirteen pouches of tobacco. They warned in Spanish against *fumar durante la lactancia*.

I was out of cigarettes. This was what I'd come upstairs for.

Next to the tobacco stood four sealed, glass jars. They were all half full of stems and flowers.

From the attic door there was a silent buzzing sound. And an artificial breeze, too. But warm, not cold.

I opened the door to the attic.

Inside were four tiny and forgotten cannabis plants in a chest-high grow tent. The grow tent was made of plastic sheeting. It was unzipped. An almost transparent blue light came from inside.

I could see the plants. They looked drooping, dehydrated, browning. My father had been dead three weeks now.

I had no idea how the plants were still alive.

I closed the attic door. Then I felt bad for the plants.

On the bookcase nearest the attic door was a watering can. Next to the watering can was some kind of tool for testing the pH of soil, and six bottles of some sort of food for plants, and an oversized horticultural syringe. And then, on the bottom shelf, was an unopened bag of purchased compost.

I took the watering can all the way downstairs to the big sink and filled it. Then I went back upstairs twice and opened the attic door again and poured some water into the soil the plants were growing in. Then I gave them all a capful of their food.

Plants drowned easy. I knew that. Especially babyish plants, like these. So I stood there a while watching, as if there was a way to take water back out of the soil if I had put too much in there.

I thought about what to do with the plants once the house was all cleaned out and sold.

I had no ideas.

So I decided not to think about that right then.

Again I had the feeling someone was watching me. I turned all around. There was nobody there. All I could hear was bird noise, and outside plants against the walls of the house, and the extractor fan hum, and the faraway sound of a nearby motorway.

I noticed that the door to the next attic—the roof area, the rafters, full of my mother and father's extremely old possessions—looked ajar. I leaned deep into the first attic and pushed it shut.

Then I shut the door to the first plant attic room as well. So the attic was all closed.

I sat on my parents' bed for a bit, staring at nothing, except my father's disgusting bathrobe, still hanging on the back of the bedroom door.

I couldn't shake the sense that I was being watched.

Once I was stoned and in my coat I walked to my grand-mother's house and knocked.

She always took a long time to answer the door because she was putting on a scarf, or something, so she would look smart.

She opened the door. She hugged me. She smelled good.

My grandmother made coffee and we sat in her living room. She sat in her chair. I sat on the sofa, close to her.

The room was dark because there were so many books in it. I liked that.

The room smelled good, like her. I worried I smelled bad. I felt too big for her house, as if I was an ugly and overgrown houseplant.

I looked around for something to say.

I said, "How's work?"

My grandmother put her hands up to her head and went arrrgkhhhh.

I grinned at her. She grinned back. Then she explained that her publisher, or someone, wanted her to write a memoir about being a teen sensation in the sixties.

She had been a teen sensation in the sixties because she was very beautiful and very, very young when her first novel came out. And because she liked to say controversial things to journalists about politics and women and the Royal Family.

"I like *Speak, Memory*," I said. "Just do it like that one."

"Good idea," she said, then grinned again. "I've just been reading his letters today."

"I didn't know he wrote to you," I said. But she didn't laugh. She just rolled her eyes.

"I don't know how one person had so many clever things to say," she said. "I have five things to say a day, if I'm lucky."

"Same," I said.

"And fewer and fewer, it seems."

"You always get there in the end," I said. She rolled her eyes but in a meaner way. I grinned.

She looked into the garden for a while. To distract her I told her about a whale that had been sighted in Norway.

The whale was wearing some kind of harness. On the harness it said PROPERTY ST. PETERSBURG.

"The Norwegians think it was a Russian spy whale. That it had been trained by the Russians to spy on people."

"Oh, no," my grandmother said. "Whale watching."

"Now it lives in a harbor in Norway. It does tricks so the Norwegians will feed it. But—"

I got distracted by my grandmother's cat. It was in her front garden eating grass with the side of its face. It had started raining slightly.

"It's good," my grandmother said, "they're feeding it."

I started laughing.

"They have to stop feeding it. So it can learn to feed itself. And then maybe make friends with some non-spy whales. A herd, or whatever."

"Civilian whales," said my grandmother. Then she started laughing, too.

We walked together to a specific field that she liked to walk to. She liked to walk to that field because sometimes there were deer in it. Usually, small women deer, but sometimes a single stag. My grandmother preferred the small women deer. She liked to stand on the first rung of the field fence and look for, then at, the deer.

She walked so slowly that I didn't know what to do with my legs. I could either take normal-sized steps in slow motion, or I could take extremely small, regular-speed steps. I alternated. It must have looked weird. I could feel myself getting less stoned.

There were no deer in the field that day. My grandmother seemed disappointed.

"They must have heard us coming," I told her.

She stood on her fence rung and kept looking just in case.

"They have their spies," she said, into the field.

"Watch out, everyone," I said, "it's those creeps who always stare at us."

She laughed.

"How did the Russians talk to the spy whale?" she said.

"In Russian," I said.

"Scandinavians are a very paranoid people," she said.

"Two whales walk into a bar," I said. "One whale goes hurrrrggggnnhhhh weeeoooooooow clik clk clk hrrrnnnggg."

"Very good," my grandmother said.

"The other whale goes: are you okay, man? You sound pretty drunk."

"Yes," my grandmother said, "very good."

I walked back via the shop. It was dark now. But I wanted proper cigarettes.

I used the torch on my phone for the parts of the path that had no streetlights. Behind me I was sure that I heard footsteps on the damp early-dropped leaves.

But when I turned around there was never anyone there.

A boy and girl stopped me before I could go in. The girl asked me to buy them cigarettes.

"Can you buy us some cigarettes?" she said. "I am eighteen. I am nineteen. But I forgot my identification."

"Alcohol, too. We are nineteen," the boy said.

They were leaning against the closed doors of a parked car.

Their voices were very quiet. But not a whisper. Just like someone had turned their volumes down, or something.

I said, "Is that your car?"

The boy turned his head slightly to look at it. The parts of the car the streetlight hit were a deep metallic blue. It looked as old as they were.

"Yeah," the girl said.

"Nice," I said.

There was no real food in the shop so I bought garlic bread, a frozen pizza, diet cola, alcohol.

The girl didn't say what brand of cigarettes she liked. So

I just bought three packs of the brand I liked. I paid and dropped them into the transparent blue plastic bag with all of the other groceries.

Outside, the girl with the turned-down voice asked me what happened to my face.

I said, "My skin keeps coming off."

"Like eczema?" the boy said. "It looks bruised."

"Yeah," I said, "someone hit me."

"Why?" said the girl.

"Do you know Cheryl? She wears purple. All the time. She hit me."

"We don't know her," the boy said.

"Right," I said. Then I handed the girl what I'd bought them.

"We don't have any money," the boy said.

"You don't have any money," I said. The girl stepped back. The boy went into his pocket.

"We have these," said the boy. He held up around three dozen red-pink Xanax bars in a transparent ziplock bag. The transparent ziplock bag was stained red-pink with the dust of the bars.

"You do not have any money," I said.

"We'll give you three of these. For the stuff."

I looked up at the sky, then at the boy.

He nudged his hand toward me as if he was the scary ghost in *Spirited Away*. Or a child attempting to feed a farm animal.

"Five," I said.

He handed me three pills loose, one by one. I could feel that the inside of my hand was sweating.

"Xanax?" I said.

"Yeah," the girl said.

"How strong?"

"Five milligrams on each bar. So do half one."

"Right," I said.

I put the bars loose in my coat. My fingernails were long and caught the lining of my pocket. I felt last year's lint in there, getting all up in with the pills.

"Don't get into any more fights," the girl said.

"You should see the other guy," I said.

"I thought you said it was a lady," the boy said.

"Yeah," I said.

I moved slightly to show I was walking away. I looked at the blue-black sky. I thought about the dark and scary path back to the house.

I said, "Can you drive me home?"

At the house I invited them in.

I made three drinks with some vodka and some diet cola and some ice. I stored the vodka in the freezer section of the fridge-freezer, which was huge, and expensive, and dispensed its own ice, like fridge-freezers did on American television shows.

The boy and the girl sat on stools at the breakfast bar.

I put the drinks in front of them. Then I bowed a bit in a butler-type way.

They said, "Thanks."

"Are you hungry?" I said. "I have fake food. Like garlic bread."

"No," the girl said, for both of them. "But thanks."

I looked around the room.

I said, "We could smoke a joint."

The boy smiled and said, "Sure."

I nodded and left the room.

I went up both sets of stairs to my parents' bedroom to collect one of my father's jars of cannabis.

While I was up there I opened the first attic to check on the plants.

They seemed less wilted, but it was hard to tell.

I thought about pouring more water on the plants. But I didn't. I didn't want to drown them.

I closed the attic back up tight.

I went back downstairs.

"Cool," the girl said. I sat down at the breakfast bar with them. Then I did finger guns at her.

"Your parents aren't in," the boy said.

I nodded. I started making a giant Rizla from several regular-sized Rizla. My fingers were cold. And they felt too damp to do a good job.

"Yeah," I said.

"Can we put the heating on?" the girl said.

I thought about it.

"I don't know," I said. The girl laughed.

"You don't know?" she said. She laughed again. I started laughing, too.

"No," I said. "I don't know how. It just comes on sometimes."

The girl laughed harder.

"Is this even your house?" the boy said. I laughed some more. I lit the joint and inhaled.

"No," I said, "I broke in. It's a secret."

The girl said, "We do that, too."

"We should team up," I said, "you can live here."

"It's too cold," the boy said. I laughed.

I inhaled more of the joint then passed it to the girl.

Halfway through the boy handed me half a red-pink pill. I chewed it to wet dust.

The vodka and diet cola and ice were too cold and my teeth hurt in my gums so I drank more.

I ashed the joint into a blue-and-white patterned dish in the center of the breakfast bar. Then I passed it back to the girl.

Later, in the bathroom, I braced my hand against a wall and stuck my finger into my throat. The muscles of my stomach jerked and warm fluid came out. As waves of it passed through my chest and belly, sour blue lumps lodged in my throat and mouth, and when I pushed them with my tongue they numbed my gums and dropped into the water.

I woke up in the bathroom when it was light. I stayed there awhile. When I felt like it I stood up and put my mouth under the cold tap. I let it run and lapped water into my mouth, like a cat.

I moved the water around my mouth. Then I spat it into the sink. It was yellow.

In the bathroom mirror, I saw yellow vomit stains on my white T-shirt.

Upstairs, in the attic, I could hear the extractor fans and some other, second wind sound, different to the sound the fans made.

At the breakfast bar I smoked a cigarette.

The dish we had been using as an ashtray was full of ash and roaches and cigarette butts. There were maybe seven used glasses on the breakfast bar too, some surrounded by small puddles of sticky-seeming dry liquid, some with half-floating cigarette ends.

I looked at my phone but there was nothing on it. Like it was broken, or dead.

The car belonging to the boy and girl was outside still. But they did not seem to be in the house anymore.

I looked around the house a little bit in case they were hiding somewhere.

I ate a quarter of one of the coffee table Xanax bars and went upstairs and slept on the bed in my childhood bedroom.

It was dark. Outside I could hear the sound of a garden animal, or something. I took off my clothes with the vomit on and went to the bathroom and showered. The fresh skin on my chest and left hand stung a little under the hot water.

I put on a T-shirt with an anthropomorphized broccoli on it. The broccoli was wearing sunglasses and doing finger guns and below him it said BRO in big black letters. On the back of the T-shirt was another broccoli, also anthropomorphized. This broccoli was wearing ski gear, and sunglasses, and the black writing this time said FRO-BRO. I put on some blue jeans and socks.

Downstairs I started cleaning. Then I gave up. Instead I opened the fridge and took a sugar-free Red Bull that was in there for some reason and drank it.

My father's study was on the ground floor of the house. My mother's study was on the first floor. They both had big windows. But there were so many books in them that they were dark inside.

I had music on that I could hear from upstairs.

In our London flat, mine and my girlfriend's, we couldn't play music loud because of the neighbors. But there were no neighbors here. Except Cheryl. But her house was far away. And she probably wouldn't be coming round again anytime soon.

My mother's study was messy. It didn't seem like my dad had cleaned it since my mother moved out of the house into the care home. Maybe he thought she wasn't done yet.

But then my study would have been a mess too, if I had one.

There were books everywhere, and loose papers, and photocopies of materials from her teaching at the university, with underlining, and notes in almost illegible handwriting. There was a very old laptop with a slightly newer printer beside it.

On the desk was a neatly stacked pile of paper. It was the only neat thing in there. I went over to it.

I had the feeling that I was being watched. But I brushed it off. I had locked all the doors.

Just in case I checked the windows. But I couldn't see any-one out there.

I lit a cigarette.

The neatly stacked pile of paper was a manuscript. It had a title page and everything. It was very white and had less dust on it than everything else in the room.

The title on the manuscript was *A Bit of Earth*.

I was full of caffeine and not-sugar from the Red Bull and didn't know what to do with myself. So I started reading it.

A Bit of Earth

Rebecca Smith

CHAPTER ONE

✦

An organ would be too loud for a child's funeral. As the pianist played *Morningtown Ride* the coffin was carried out, tiny and horribly small. He was a slight boy. He couldn't have made it past three stone.

> *Maybe it is raining*
> *where our train shall ride,*
> *all the little travelers are warm and snug inside...*

I stopped reading. I stood up and moved around the room a little bit. I remembered my mother singing that song to me softly on night drives back from visiting relatives, both of us in the back seat, my dad driving and my brother sometimes up front with him, me drifting in and out of sleep with my head on my mother's shoulder or in her lap.

I thought about how that was the song she would probably have played at my funeral, if I'd died then.

She must have thought about it or she wouldn't have written it. But I guessed that was probably a normal thing for mothers to think about.

I moved around the room a bit more.

I checked the window.

Then I sat back down and started reading again.

✤

An organ would be too loud for a child's funeral. As the pianist played *Morningtown Ride* the coffin was carried out, tiny and horribly small. He was a slight boy. He couldn't have made it past four stone.

Maybe it is raining
where our train shall ride,
all the little travelers are warm and snug inside...

There were flower arrangements of a yellow digger and the White Rabbit from *Alice in Wonderland*, with a watch that had now stopped forever. The sun streamed through the stained glass, casting lozenges of light in sweet-wrapper colors across the flagstones.

Rebecca woke, clutching at her pillow, finding that here it was sunshine and day. She lurched out of bed and across the landing to Felix and Joanna's bedroom. They were asleep, and the sunshine could not penetrate the curtains she had made for their windows. They had thermal as well as blackout linings. She gently sat down at the end of Felix's bed and picked up Marmalade, his toy cat.

Rebecca and Felix and Joanna were never late for nursery. They took a shortcut across the university, past the Department of Medicine, often walking that far with Daddy, whose name was Guy. He was Doctor Guy Misselthwaite, Head of Dermatology in the Medicine department.

I read quickly. In the manuscript, Rebecca dropped her children off at nursery. She needed to buy polo shirts for Felix, the boy, who was starting school imminently. So she walked to a bus stop and waited for a bus to take her into the city center.

＋

As Rebecca reached the bus stop, after leaving Felix and Joanna at the nursery, she saw a bus pulling away. No matter: she had plenty of time. Another bus would arrive soon. She could get round the shops and be back in time to collect Felix and Joanna. She was the only person waiting at the bus stop. Perhaps it was worth having missed that bus to avoid waiting with a group of students.

Rebecca saw Professor Lovage, History of Art, walking toward her, smiling and swinging her bag in a girlish, carefree way. Rebecca smiled back.

"Off into town?" Professor Lovage asked.

"Felix needs a few things for starting school. White polo shirts."

"A big step. Is he looking forward to it?"

"I don't know; he doesn't seem to have much of a sense of time, so I don't think he thinks about it that much. Some of the children from his nursery that he knows are going too, though."

"That'll make it easier. I'm sure he'll be all right. He's such a charming boy."

Rebecca smiled.

"Thank you. He is. I've no idea where he learned it."

"Don't be silly," Professor Lovage said. She raised her eyebrows and smiled. "Good luck with the shopping."

She continued in the direction she was going, leaving Rebecca alone at the bus stop. A moment later, a car of astonishing beauty pulled up beside Rebecca: an Alfa Romeo in deep and metallic Mediterranean blue. The top was down. Rebecca saw that the driver was Julius East, Head of Spanish.

"Where are you going, Rebecca?"

"Shopping," she said, smiling.

"Fancy a lift?"

She paused, too polite to accept eagerly, too polite to refuse.

"I'm sure my bus will be along soon."

"You prefer a bus to this?"

He smiled at her slowly, knowing that she would accept. She stood there on the pavement a moment, unsure, until Julius got out of the car, leaving the engine running, and stepped around it to open the passenger-side door. It had been a while since anyone had done that for her.

The seats were made of the softest leather Rebecca had ever felt. She suspected that there was some glossy showroom brochure name for the color of them. Tan seemed too pedestrian. And what kind of animal had it once been?

"Relax," Julius said. "You have your knees all pulled up. You're hugging them as though you're a schoolgirl. Perhaps you are. You do look so young."

"Oh, I'm really very old," Rebecca said. But she stretched out her legs. "This is a beautiful car."

"It's new. We'll take a detour. So you can see what it's really like."

As Julius accelerated, Rebecca's hair whipped into her eyes. It might be turned to string by the time they arrived. She pushed it behind her ears again and again.

"In there," he indicated the glove compartment with a slight thrust of his chin, "there's a scarf you can borrow."

The scarf was a long thin rectangle of heavy white silk. She placed it over her head and knotted it at the nape of her neck, wondering who it belonged to. Perhaps Julius just kept it there for whatever woman (or, more likely, pretty student) he happened to pick up. She could feel his eyes on her legs. She placed her bag primly on her knees. She did not like feeling watched.

They were in the forest now. She wondered when they would turn back.

"I have to get some polo shirts. For Felix. My son. He's starting school."

"You will have plenty of time on your hands," he said.

Rebecca looked down at her hands crossed over her bag in her lap as if she might see time growing there, a silky golden fur. Or perhaps it would be thyme, with little stalks coiling around her fingers. She imagined pulling it out from the skin of her hands, stem by stem.

But Rebecca's hands were unchanged, pink, slim and neat. She had a French manicure. The idea of having your nails painted to look like nails pleased her.

"The sky is bluer out here, don't you think?" she said, gazing upward. There were three airplanes leaving wonderful paths across the sky. "Once, when Felix saw some of the vapor trails, he said: 'Mummy, the clouds are lining up!'"

Julius East smiled. Rebecca could tell that he was smiling. But she didn't look across. She just kept looking up. And that was why Rebecca didn't see the deer, or know that Julius was going to swerve to avoid it. She never knew what happened.

I threw up the sugar-free Red Bull into the bathroom sink. I managed not to get any on my T-shirt this time.

The vomit was thin and watery and smelled strongly of Red Bull.

It stung my lips and the inside of my nose.

I wondered when was the last time I had eaten anything.

I ran the tap to wash it away. Then I ran water around my mouth. Then I brushed my teeth, swallowing a little water at the end to get the remaining vomit back down my throat.

I lit a cigarette and looked at myself in the mirror. The bruising on my face was fading now, forming an almost transparent blue-green blotch on my face, shining through my pink skin like sunlight through stained glass.

In the attic the plants looked healthier now. They were drooping less. They were standing up more straight. They looked like they had grown a little. I felt good about that.

I closed the attic and sat down on my parents' bed and looked at the internet on my phone for guides on caring for the plants. That seemed better than killing them. Or letting them die. And I would get more drugs if they turned to flowers.

From the guides and from how the plants looked and from the settings on the timer attached to the ultraviolet light I deduced that the plants were early in their life cycle. They were young and thirsty.

I found a spray bottle on a different bookshelf and put a capful of the plant food in it. Then I went downstairs to the big sink and filled the spray bottle with water from the tap. Then I went back to the attic and misted all of the young plants with the mixture individually, liberally.

That night I was on a date with a girl in a windowless basement bar. Not my girlfriend. Some slightly wider, blonder, shorter girl.

We were maybe two drinks in. Me standing at a high table, her perched on a stool for ladies.

I looked down.

I saw I was dressed Winnie-the-Pooh style: an orange T-shirt, but no trousers or underwear or shoes.

I thought to myself: style it out, style it out.

So I said: oh, bother.

Then I woke up.

When I left the house the car that seemed to belong to the boy and girl was still there.

I noticed that a few house roof tiles had fallen, smashed to pieces on the gravel below.

I worried about rain getting in. But I didn't know what I could do about that.

I just started walking to the care home they kept my mother in.

My mother was sitting in her disgusting chair. I bent to hug her. Then I sat down opposite in a chair that was plastic and stackable. It made a bad sound when it moved against the floor.

"What happened to your face?" my mother said, to me.

"Nothing," I said. "Nothing happened. My face is fine."

I looked around for something to say before I asked her about the manuscript. Then I remembered the Russian spy whale. So I told her about that.

"The Norwegians think it was a Russian spy whale. That it had been trained by the Russians to spy on people."

"Oh, no," my mother said.

"Now it lives in a harbor in Norway. It does tricks so the Norwegians will feed it."

"That's good. They're feeding it."

"They have to stop. So it can learn to feed itself. And make friends with some normal whales."

"Civilian whales," my mother said. She smiled to herself and looked out of the window. Then she looked back at me.

"What?" I said. But she didn't hear me.

"It's so nice to see you," she said. "I saw a deer from the window yesterday."

She nodded slowly at the window. It faced onto a busy road. I hoped she was confused. Or misremembering.

"Right," I said.

"What?" she said.

"In your study," I said, "there's a manuscript."

"I don't have a study. This is a care home."

"At the house. Not here. Your study in the house."

"The house must be very valuable now," she said. "We paid the whole mortgage. You should sell it."

"There's a manuscript in the study there. Were you writing a book? Before you came here. Dad didn't say anything about it. You finished a book?"

My mother twisted her face up. I was talking too fast for her. So I stopped.

"I don't know," she said.

"It's important, Mum," I said.

"I'm sorry," she said.

"A woman dies at the beginning. A mother. In a car crash. You gave the character your name."

My mother kept her face twisted up. It made me feel bad to see her do that.

"I don't remember," she said. "I wrote this? What happens after?"

"I don't know. I wanted to talk to you about it. Before I read any more."

"What?"

"If you wrote a book I want people to read it," I said, "it's important. But I wanted to ask you about it first."

My mother untwisted her face. But she did not look relieved. She looked down at her thin and swollen hands. She moved them about slightly. She looked very, very sad.

"I was going to write so many books," she said.

Why did you say you'd finished writing it if you hadn't even started?" my brother said, on the phone. I'd just come clean to him.

"I don't know," I said.

"You're retarded," my brother said, "I am amazed they let retards like you write books."

I said, "You'd be surprised."

"Just be honest," he said.

"I guess they heard about Dad. Because they haven't emailed in a little while. He bought me some time."

"You're retarded. My wife wants to talk to you."

"Makes sense," I said.

"Gabriel," my brother's wife said, "how are you?"

"Good," I said.

It was around four in the afternoon. I was pretty sure it was Sunday. I had been asleep when the third call woke me. Lying on my back, now, I could feel imprints from the sofa fabric on my face. My mouth tasted like ash. The back of my throat felt all clogged.

My brother was a lot older than me. He and his wife got married when they were at university because she was pregnant. They had a son. He was my nephew.

My grandmother had had my mother when she was very young. And my mother had had me when she was very old.

Sometimes it felt like our whole family was in the wrong order, or something.

"How is the clear-out going?" my brother's wife said.

"The clear-out?" I said.

"Of the house. You are clearing out the house."

"Yes, I am," I said. "It's going well. I'm worried about the house, though. Some roof tiles fell down."

"Roof tiles?"

"And the plants are growing fast outside. Like, the weeds."

"Do some gardening. What did you say about roof tiles?"

"Nothing, don't worry," I said, worrying that they'd send someone to fix them. And then I'd have to deal with all that.

I said, "It's all going really well."

"That's so great," she said. She was using her business voice. It made me feel stupid. "We've asked an estate agent to do a valuation. They'll be round this week. Your brother will call again with the specifics."

"All right," I said.

"We thought we'd drive down. Maybe this weekend or the weekend after. You should be almost done by then. We can go through the things."

"Arrgkhhhh," I said.

"What?"

"I said: all right," I said.

Once they were off the phone I went on my laptop and looked again at my girlfriend's story, about the oligarch and the paintings.

I scrolled all the way down to the author photo I didn't recognize.

Then I scrolled around the story a bit more.

It made me feel the same kind of bad as before.

I ate some of the pink Xanax off the coffee table. I got a cold bottle of white wine from the fridge and took it to the bathroom. I smelled bad. I ran a bath.

I lay in the bath for a while and waited for the bar to kick. A layer of condensation formed on the wine bottle.

Once the bathwater was coldening—after the Xanax had kicked in and I'd drunk maybe a third of the bottle—I tried to masturbate.

My penis felt loose.

When I raised it above the waterline I saw that the skin on it was coming away.

I pulled at the dead skin.

It was tender and it came away in small pieces.

I tore away the entire skin around my crotch, penis, and upper thighs.

The tiny pieces of me floated in the bathwater.

I got out of the bath and drained it. I finished the bottle of wine while drying my new and remaining skin.

I was cold and I was not wearing any clothes. My hair was still wet. My phone said 4 a.m.

I didn't know how long I'd been asleep. The bottle of wine was beside me, empty.

I heard the television say, downstairs: *number seventeen on our list of twenty common misconceptions about the end of the world.*

I didn't remember turning it on.

Upstairs, in the attic, I could hear the extractor fans working overtime.

I put on a T-shirt that said RICKIE LAMBERT IS DA BEST and went to check the plants. I didn't put trousers or underwear on. My skin felt too tender.

The house was dark and I did not turn on the landing light. Or the lights in my parents' bedroom. My father's disgusting bathrobe touched me on the arm as their bedroom door closed behind me.

The blue glow from under the first attic door meant that the grow lights were on. Which meant my father had programmed the timer wrong, maybe. It seemed bad that the lights were on in the night. The plants would be confused. Or maybe they wouldn't be.

Inside the attic, inside the grow tent, the plants seemed

fine. They were much bigger now. Almost a foot tall. They were growing so fast.

I misted them lightly with the solution I'd made. I wanted to ask them if they were confused by the lights being on at nighttime.

But that was how the timer was set. It seemed better not to change anything.

What did I know about growing things?

I noticed that the door to the second attic was ajar. I was sure that I had closed it before. But now it was definitely open. And there was a cold draft coming from it. Maybe from the fallen roof tiles I had seen in the garden.

I did not want the plants to get cold.

I had never been into the second attic, really. It was dark and scary. I was scared. But I wanted to see what was in it.

I pulled the door to it open more. The draft got bigger and colder. The air smelled different, damper, badder.

I moved my body around the grow tent. I edged into the second attic. I found a light switch in the dark and switched it.

The lightbulb still worked. I did not know the last time someone had been up in here.

Everywhere was boxes, bits of small furniture, paintings leaned against walls, books, dust-filled cobwebs.

In the bulb-light I saw black mold growing on the attic walls. It seemed bad.

Outside plants were growing in through the roof, somehow.

I tried not to inhale. Maybe there were bats living here. Bat droppings could make you sick. I knew that.

My feet were bare on the dusty floor. I thought about nails I might step on. I did not want a rusty nail in my foot. I worried about the attic-dust-air on the skin of my exposed penis, too. I did not want to get a dust allergy on my penis. I was very allergenic. I did not want to break out.

Again I had the feeling someone was watching me. I looked back out of the attic, through the grow tent area, into my parents' bedroom. But it was too dark to see anything.

There was nobody in the attic. Nobody I could see.

I held my breath. I did not want to breathe in.

I didn't want to touch anything, either. It all looked boring and dusty. I really did not want to have to clean it all out.

But I picked up one shoebox. It had REBECCA written on it, in black permanent marker, in handwriting that looked like my mother's.

I shook the shoebox slightly so some of the dust slipped off. I heard a heavy plastic sound in it.

I looked around the attic again. Everything was still dusty and boring and scary. But I thought I would take that box downstairs.

So I got out of the second attic into the first attic and made sure the door to the second attic was shut very properly. So my plants wouldn't get cold.

I took the shoebox all the way downstairs to the living room.

The television was on. It was set to the History Channel. It was showing a program about the various deaths of Nelson Mandela. I turned it off.

I turned the light on. I opened the box.

Inside was a videotape and some photographs and a small and ornate mirror and various pieces of brown and amber jewelry. A trapped insect in one of the necklaces.

I spread it all out on the coffee table and sat on the floor in front of it. I still didn't have any trousers or underwear on. I could feel the hairs on my new skin standing.

The photos were of my mother as a teenager.

She was with my grandmother and with her sisters and with people who I assumed were her friends. They had big hair and old clothes. The photos were dark and badly lit. Sometimes people were smiling and sometimes they were posing, not smiling, with eyeliner and hands against walls.

I looked at the videotape. It was in a tacky metallic-blue slip. I slipped it out.

I turned the television back on. There was a VHS player attached, still, so my father could watch his collection of old television shows and movies. For research or because he was bored or both.

I put the videotape into the player and rewound it. It made a sound I'd not heard in a long time. I sat cross-legged on the floor so I could control the player.

I pressed play.

At first there was just VHS snowstorm. Then a picture

appeared. I recognized the legs as my mother's. The camera pointed into her lap. I heard her say: *okay, it's started, it's beginning.*

The camera moved around the room. I recognized the house as this one. There was my father, sat beside her. He made a funny face into the camera. My mother laughed. My father grinned.

The camera pointed in a new direction. I saw my brother but very young, moving colored shapes around an impossibly curved and useless abacus. *Look*, my mother said, *you're on video.* My brother looked confused and then came toward the camera grinning, but looking at my mother behind the camera, not into the camera at all.

The snowstorm reappeared and then a new image. My mother holding the camera again. But now in my brother's bedroom, before it was a study. My father shirtless, holding my brother in one arm, painting the walls of the bedroom. Just the sound of the camcorder whirring. My father turning to the camera and smiling sheepishly.

I paused the tape on that. The image stayed still and carouseled up and down.

I looked at my flickering dad for the longest time.

Then I pressed play again.

The snowstorm reappeared and stayed there. I thought about stopping the tape and rewinding it. I wanted to see my family again. But I wanted to see if there was anything else on the tape, too.

Eventually the snowstorm shifted into an image. At first it was too light and fucked to see anything properly. But then I saw my mother again. Older now, older than earlier in the video. Old enough that I recognized her from when I was a child. She was sitting on the bonnet of a metallic-blue Alfa Romeo Spider. The person holding the camera walked toward her. Whoever was holding it was tall. My mother put her hand up to the camera and laughed.

Snowstorm reappeared on the screen.

I looked around the room. I noticed light from the television reflecting off the small ornate mirror that had been in the shoebox. It bounced around the room somehow.

Another image appeared out of the snow.

It was my mother again, the same age, outdoors, sitting on a picnic blanket with a man I did not recognize. The camera was being held at child-height, moving more than it should. I could barely make out the man sitting beside my mother. He looked big and thin and Spanish or South American. My body started to feel bad and full of movement.

The image cut to something else. There was minimal snowstorm this time, almost none. It was my mother again, a third time, the same age, embracing two smiling children. The children looked roughly the same age as each other. They looked familiar. But I did not recognize them. In the background was the same metallic-blue car as in the video before.

The video ended there.

I rewound it. I saw my father again. Then my mother with the car. And my mother with the big and thin Spanish or South American man. Then my mother embracing the smiling boy and girl.

I let the video stop.

I lit a cigarette and stood. My head rushed like unwinding.

I walked over to the huge and faded gold-framed mirror that hung on the wall of the living room. In my hand was the small ornate mirror from the shoebox. I stood in front of the huge mirror and held up the small mirror to it. I put my head in between the two mirrors. I tried to look into the big mirror to see the smaller mirror reflected back into it.

But the small mirror was too small and my head was too big and it was too dark to see anything anyway.

Before I went back to sleep I tried to masturbate. My body felt bad and full of movement. I wanted to make that stop. And I wanted to see if my penis still worked after losing the skin on it.

I got hard. But I felt sensitive when I touched myself slightly, and it stung badly when I put my hand around myself and moved my foreskin up and down.

I gave up and passed out.

I woke to the sound of the landline ringing.

I looked at my actual phone. There were missed calls from my brother on it.

I waited for the landline to ring out.

I heard my dad's voice say to leave a message. I thought about not calling my brother back. But I did.

"He speaks," my brother said.

"What do you want?" I said, in a Robert De Niro mafia-guy voice. I took the phone away from my ear while my brother was talking to look at the clock on it. It said 1 p.m.

"What?" I said, when my phone was back on my ear.

"Were you asleep?"

"I was out."

"Sure," my brother said. "The estate agent is coming the day after tomorrow. To do a valuation."

"Evaluate what?" I said.

"A valuation. How's the clear-out going?"

"I found a VHS," I said, "in the attic."

"The attic? You must be almost done, then."

"It has Mum and Dad and you in it. The video. But also Mum with another family, I think."

"He's coming at two. The day after tomorrow. Make sure everything looks valuable."

"I don't know who the other family is. In the video. With Mum. I don't know if I can ask her. It's a whole other family."

"I heard a story you'll like," my brother said. "A friend of mine works in the Job Centre. In the town where the house is. He had to tell a man that they were stopping his benefits. So he'd need to get a job.

"And the man whose benefits they're stopping, he looks at my friend. Then he looks around. Then he clutches his chest, where his heart is, and he falls off the chair.

"And he just lies there, on the ground. Dead of a heart attack, or something. So my friend rushes out of his little office to get help."

"Oh, no," I said.

"And the first person he sees, he says: this guy, he just died in my office.

"And the person says: was it Frank Thingy?

"And my friend goes: yeah. I think he's dead.

"And the person just shakes their head and starts laughing. And my friend is panicking now, saying they need to call an ambulance, call for medical support, whatever. Because the guy is dead."

"Oh, no," I said.

"Yeah, so. My friend is panicking and the more he panics the more the other person laughs. And my friend is getting really worried now. Because this person is hysterical with laughter. But there is a dead guy in my friend's office.

"So the person eventually stops laughing and takes my friend by the arm and walks him back to his office. And they just stand there watching the guy. From the doorway of the office. And they just stand there watching him. And my friend is panicking, but eventually he notices that the guy is still breathing.

"And his colleague laughs again, and says: get up, Frank.

"And Frank—who was dead—gets up, and doesn't look at them, and kind of dusts himself down, and then sits back down in the chair."

"Oh," I said.

"Yeah. So apparently this guy just does that. Plays dead when he hears something he doesn't like. That's his thing. He's known for it."

"Pretending," I said.

"Yeah. Pretending to be dead. Whenever he hears something he doesn't like."

"Like if an estate agent came to value his childhood home?" I said.

"Or if his dickhead brother fucked up a house sale that could make him a lot of money," my brother said.

"I don't like that story," I said.

"Yeah, you do. You love it. You dirty little slut."

"I've got to go, I'm dying," I said, and hung up the phone.

I just sat there on my childhood bed awhile staring into nothing. It had started raining slightly outside. I could hear it. I liked the sound it made. I opened the window so I could hear it better and heard the sound of the motorway too, far away.

Downstairs I heard the television say: *welcome to the money-wellness revolution.*

The rain made the air coming through the window cold and I put the quilt from the bed around my shoulders.

Then I heard a different sound. From out the window. Like the sound of a garden animal but larger. So I looked out the window properly. But I couldn't see anything there.

I heard the sound again. It seemed to be coming from the old and fucked-up garden shed.

I knelt on the bed to look out of the window.

I saw the door to the shed open on its almost broken hinges.

The sound was the man. The figure I'd seen before. But he was not dressed as a man. I couldn't see what he was dressed as at first.

The man came out of the garden shed holding a pair of oversized rust-covered shears.

He pushed the door to the shed closed behind him.

I shouted.

And the man turned to the window slowly. And that's when I saw what he was dressed as.

The man was dressed in a horrible mud-covered brown costume.

The costume had its own fur. The fur was full of dried mud and attached plant matter, leaves, twigs, matted.

And on his head he had a mask of a deer face. A woman deer, without antlers. Covering his whole head.

I couldn't see eyeholes in the deer mask. Just glassy mask eyes. Far too far apart for him to see out of.

He stood there in the light rain looking at me in the window for a moment, still holding the rusted shears in one of his brown-gloved hands.

I wanted to shout again. But I didn't. We just stayed there looking at each other.

Then the man turned back toward the shed and opened the door to it. Then he looked back at me. Then he went into the shed and I heard the sound of tools in it.

Then I saw him come out of the shed. I shouted again.

I noticed he didn't have the shears anymore.

He closed the door to the shed without turning back to the window.

Then the man clomped off toward the trees at the end of the garden until I couldn't see him anymore.

I stayed at the window watching for a long time to see if the deer-man came back.

But he didn't.

So I put on dirty clothes, still watching the window.

I went downstairs to the kitchen. I took a big knife out of the knife block. Like I had before.

I thought about calling the police. But the house was full of drugs. And I wasn't a snitch.

I looked out of the kitchen window into the garden. It was still raining slightly. The door to the shed was slightly open.

I put a cigarette in my mouth and lit it.

I opened the back door and took my knife out into the garden.

I shouted a sound with the cigarette still in my mouth. I wanted to keep my hands free.

I couldn't hear anything.

I looked around everywhere and started walking down the long garden to the shed. I kept my eyes really wide.

At the shed, I stood away from it and pulled the door open with my non-knife hand. Just in case the deer-man had snuck back in there and was waiting to jump me with the rusted hedge trimmers, or another garden implement.

The shed was empty.

I heard a sound from the trees at the bottom of the garden.

I didn't shout this time. I stepped back from the shed farther. I walked quietly toward the trees.

At the trees there were no more sounds. And I couldn't see anything, either. But the trees at the end of the garden turned into a dense-ish patch of woodland.

There was a fucked-up wire fence showing where the garden ended. It had been broken in one place. So you could easily jump it.

I stood looking into the woodland. The sound of rain on remaining leaves; birds.

I looked up at the biggest tree. I knew it was an ash. It had some kind of lesion on it. It looked dying.

I stood there with my knife a long time, moving my head around and shifting between feet quietly. But there were no more sounds. So eventually I gave up.

I went back to the house. On the way I looked into the shed again.

The shed was weirdly clean. I had been expecting more cobwebs. But there weren't many. All the garden tools were neatly arranged. The shears had been returned. They were in their spot.

I closed the door to the shed and went back to the house.

I found a padlock with a key in it in the drawer of stuff.

I took the padlock out to the shed and locked the door shut tight.

I turned to go back into the house. The house looked so fucked up. Plants were growing all up it, flaking bricks. Holes in the roof where tiles had fallen.

The walls were beginning to peel.

I went back into it.

I checked again that all the house doors were locked properly. And that the windows were closed, too.

I took half a Xanax and sat on my bed cross-legged. I watched the window and waited.

I tried to ignore the front door, but when I opened it the boy and girl were standing there. The boy stood at the front. The girl stood behind him, swinging car keys around her finger.

"Hi," I said.

"You've got vomit on you," the boy said, all quiet.

"Your car is here," I said, nodding at the car.

"We came to pick it up."

I invited them inside. Then I told them the story about a man who pretends to be dead.

"That's a sad story," the girl said. The boy nodded and passed the girl the joint I had just rolled.

"How come your parents are never home?"

"They're dead," I said. "This is my house now."

"Our parents are dead, too," the boy said. "In a car crash."

"Your car looks fine," I said.

"Your house looks fucked up," the girl said. "The front of it is all crumbling."

"Are you brother and sister?" I said. They looked at each other.

"Yeah," the girl said.

"Where do you live?"

"We told you," the boy said, "nowhere."

"Right," I said.

"Yeah," the girl said.

"I want to show you something," I said.

We went into the living room and I showed them the blue oriental-looking vase that had my father's ash in it. My mother's possessions and the blue slip of the videotape were still all over the coffee table.

The girl said, "Have you touched the ash?"

In the mirror behind the vase I saw the girl sit down on the floor in front of the coffee table, where I'd been sitting before. She started looking at the photographs and jewelry. She picked up the amber insect and held it to the light.

She said, "This thing is fucked."

"Look at this," I said. I turned the television on and went over to the VHS player. I made sure the tape was at the start of itself. Then I pressed play.

"What is this?" the boy said.

"Watch it," I told them.

The images appeared on-screen. My mother's lap. Then my father, making his face. Then my brother but young, running toward the camera, grinning.

"That's you?" the girl said, quiet.

"My brother," I said.

"Your dad was handsome," she said.

I said, "Yeah."

Snowstorm filled the screen. The tape changed. The too-bright light. Then the image of my mother leaning on the car, laughing, holding her hand up to the camera.

"It's the same car as yours," I said.

The boy and girl didn't say anything. The tape cut again to snowstorm. I looked around at them.

"You saw the car?" I said.

The boy looked like he was about to cry. The girl just looked angry.

The tape cut again, to my mother on the picnic blanket with the big and thin Spanish or South American man, the camera at child-height.

"Fuck this," the girl said, so quiet I almost didn't hear.

She got up and left the room. The boy followed. The tape cut to snowstorm again.

"You should see this," I half-shouted.

I heard the front door open then close. Then car doors. Then the engine starting and tires on gravel.

I didn't know what to do. So I just sat there, waiting for the tape to cut again to my smiling mother embracing the children.

But it didn't. It just stayed on the black and white and gray nothing until the tape stopped and the room had no noise in it. Or anything at all.

I heard more tiles fall from the roof. A shattering sound.

When the estate agent arrived I was asleep. I thought about not letting them in. They knocked on the door three times. But I knew that my brother would be angry if I did not let them in. So I went downstairs and opened the door.

"Wrong house," I said, "sorry."

The estate agent was tall and thin and young. Maybe younger than me. He was wearing a suit. His estate agent car was parked where the boy and girl's car was parked before. Inside, the television said: *a combined formula of seventeen ingredients designed to combat aging in normal skin.*

"I'm sorry if I'm disturbing you," he said, "I'm from Barnard Marcus. We have a visit scheduled."

I didn't say anything for a long time.

"For the valuation," he said.

"I don't know any Marcuses," I said.

"That's the company name. That's not my name."

"I think you have the wrong address," I said.

"No," he said, "I have the right address."

Inside I followed him while he walked around the house. He valued the downstairs first. He had a small iPad that he used to take photographs and tap information into. In the hallway he took a picture of paint flaking off a wall, leaving a little pile of shards of house below it.

I'd not noticed it before. It looked recent.

He bent and touched a small electronic box against the skirting board below where the paint was coming off. Something lit up red on the box.

"What's that?" I said.

"This measures water levels in walls. Damp."

"Right," I said, "damp."

We went into the kitchen. It smelled more of cannabis and cigarette smoke than the rest of the house. There were ashtrays and empty alcohol containers on the counters, small spillages. He didn't notice, or pretended not to notice. I got a cold beer out of the expensive fridge.

"You want a beer?" I said.

"No, thanks," he said.

"Do people get the fridge when they buy a house? Or do you have to bring your own fridge?"

"Usually people will bring their own fridge," he said.

"This is an expensive fridge. Write that down. Write 'expensive fridge,'" I said.

"I am not going to write that," he said.

"You know there's a housing crisis?" I said.

He didn't say anything. He just took more photos on the iPad.

"This could be a bedroom," he said, in my father's study. I had barely been in there. It was dark because the curtains were closed. There were piles of papers and an empty ashtray on the large dark-wood desk. The estate agent sniffed the air.

"Fungus," he said, to himself.

We went upstairs.

My parents had converted my brother's bedroom into my mother's study. But they'd left my bedroom as-was. I did not know how to interpret that.

Probably they didn't think about it the same way I thought about it.

"This is your bedroom?" he said. He looked around at all my childhood and teenage stuff, still there.

"What's it to you?" I said, in the Robert De Niro mafia-guy voice.

"What?"

"Nothing," I said. I took a long drink from the beer.

"And there's a third floor?" he said.

"No," I said, "no third floor."

"I saw the stairs," he said.

"So why'd you ask?"

"Look," he said, "I know selling a house is an emotional time. Especially if it was your childhood home."

He gestured around the bedroom.

"So what?" I said.

"But you need to let me do my job," he said.

"Do your job," I said, "you fucking parasite."

What the fuck?" my brother said, later, on the phone. "Seriously, what the fuck?"

"He hit me first," I said.

"He said you did not hit him at all," my brother said. "He said you missed."

"That's bullshit," I said. My head hurt from hitting the wall and then the floor when I fell. "I got a couple of good ones in. In the melee."

"And he said the house was not clean," said my brother's wife, who was on the phone too, somehow. "Fucking Jesus," she said. "Fucking Jesus. I am so angry. What the fuck have you been doing this whole time?"

"He hit me first," I said. "We should sue them. We should sue Marcus."

"They should sue us. They should sue you. Jesus fucking Christ. We are going to have to find another agent."

"Oh, no," I said.

"What the fuck have you been doing this whole time?"

After they stopped shouting at me I wrote an email to my agent. I wrote that the draft was almost done. I just needed a little pruning time. And they would receive it very shortly, but I couldn't put an exact time frame on it.

My nose caught some kind of damp sulfur, house-smell. I lit a cigarette to cover it.

They emailed back within ten minutes saying, awesome, that's great to hear, can't wait to see what you've put together, and sorry for your loss by the way.

I thought my grandmother might be out, or asleep. But when she opened the door she was just wearing an elaborate scarf.

"A nice surprise," she said. I smelled recent perfume.

We sat in her living room. Her television said: *AA: the future of breakdown, today.* She turned it off.

"I got in a fight with the estate agent," I said, pointing at the new cuts and bruising on my face. "My brother and his wife are very cross with me."

"Are you hurt?" my grandmother said.

"Not really. I got some good ones in, too. In the melee," I said. She almost laughed, then made her face stern.

"Good," she said, "you shouldn't sell that house."

"No," I said, but in a question voice.

"Estate agents are parasites," she said.

"That's what I told him," I said.

She laughed finally. Then she grinned. Then she looked into the middle distance.

"You seem a little tired," I said. I knew she took a flask of coffee to bed with her each night. I wasn't sure how many hours she slept.

"Thanks," she said. "At night, my bed keeps sliding across my bedroom floor. I don't know why. I think something's wrong with the frame."

"Do you want me to look at it?" I said.

"No," she said, "it's okay. Thank you."

"I was looking at a home video, yesterday," I said. "And old photographs. I found them in the attic."

"Any of me?" she said.

"It was of Mum when she was young. Dad, too. But then on the video there's another family that I don't recognize."

"I don't know anything about that," my grandmother said.

"What? Anything about what? The other family?" I said. She looked away. She gestured at the window.

"About anything," she said, "I don't have all the answers."

That was a family joke so I smiled despite myself. My great-grandmother had said it all the time, when she was demented.

"There are kids in the video. They look like these kids I met. A boy and girl. And they got angry when I showed them the tape. And there's another man, too. I think he's their dad. But I haven't met him."

"I have some biscuits," my grandmother said, "I just remembered. Let me get some biscuits."

She stood up and left the room slowly and barely looking at me.

I sat for a moment then followed her into the kitchen.

"And Mum was writing this book. About another family. The video was all hidden in the attic. And she didn't tell anyone about the book. The character has her name."

"What do you want?" my grandmother said, into a cupboard.

"I don't understand," I said, "I want answers."

She exhaled. She took two packets of biscuits from the

cupboard and then turned around and came over to me and hugged me. I was surprised. But I hugged her back.

She put her hands on each of my arms. She smiled. Her face very close to my chest.

"I don't have the answer you are looking for," she said, "I know it's all so upsetting. But I do have Pink Panthers, or Custard Creams."

We didn't talk any more about it.

Back at the house it was getting dark. The outside wall-plants seemed to be even bigger, like they were growing faster.

I went upstairs to my mother's study.

Again I caught a damp house-smell with my nose.

I turned on the light but it was still dark in there.

On the walls, I saw mold glowing black, growing into a dim sub-pattern.

The air felt full of bad water.

I turned the manuscript back to page one. I put the tape beside the manuscript on the desk.

Then I started reading from the beginning again.

A Bit of Earth

Rebecca Smith

CHAPTER ONE

+

An organ would be too loud for a child's funeral. As the pianist played "In Dreams" the coffin was carried out, tiny and horribly small. He was a slight boy. He couldn't have made it past five stone.

A candy-colored clown they call the sandman
Tiptoes to my room every night . . .

I stopped reading. The manuscript wasn't right. It had changed. The last time I'd read it, the song had been "Morningtown Ride."

No way my mum would have chosen something as hacky or scary as "In Dreams."

I kept reading, skipping ahead a little bit.

+

Rebecca was never late dropping Felix and Joanna off at nursery. Daddy drove them, dropping them off before continuing on to the Department of Spanish at the University. Daddy's name was Julius. He was Dr. Julius East, Head of Spanish in the Modern Languages department. He drove a metallic-blue Alfa Romeo Spider.

I stopped reading again. I stood up and then sat back down and then looked at it again. It had definitely changed.

The dad hadn't been Dr. Julius East before. The dad had been Guy something. And he hadn't taught Spanish. He had taught Dermatology. And he had walked around. Julius was the guy who drove the car and picked up Rebecca and crashed it.

I felt bad and nauseous and full of movement. I could feel my heart pushing my chest. I lit a cigarette. I started reading again.

+

At the bus stop, Rebecca saw a person she recognized walking toward her. It was Dr. Guy Misselthwaite, Head of Dermatology in the Medicine department.

It was a cruel irony that Guy was Head of Dermatology. Or maybe it wasn't. Guy fought a seemingly endless battle of his own with eczema and acne, the two somehow coexisting on his own face and hands and scalp. Rebecca had seen Guy at a barbershop once, in town, the poor barber grimacing while attempting to shave around the pus- and blood-filled sores on the back of Guy's weird and oversized head.

Why did Guy not simply cut his own hair?

Guy limped up to her.

"Rebecca," he said, "what are you doing? Where are you going? Into town?"

He spat at her slightly as he talked. Rebecca stepped back. He seemed to have a different speech impediment each time they spoke. Rebecca dreaded to think about all the cruel jokes his students secretly made at his expense.

"Yes," Rebecca said, "Felix needs some white polo shirts."

"For school? Is he that old already?" Guy stepped toward her again. He squinted at her in the sun with his puffy and slightly bloodshot eyes. They were almost exactly the same height. But Guy must have weighed at least twice as much as her. Rebecca looked away, into the sun then out of it.

"Time flies," she said. She willed time to fly, her bus to arrive.

They stood there in silence for a moment. Guy sniffed. His sinuses sounded full of something. Rebecca realized that she wanted to be kind to him.

"How's your day going, Guy? Are you working on anything interesting?" she said. She used the rhythm of her speech to take another step backward. She could smell his breath on her.

"Actually," he said, "something fascinating for once. This fascinating patient. It's unlike anything I've ever seen before. Or my colleagues. We've never seen anything like it."

"Really," Rebecca said.

"They—I won't go into medical detail. They shed their skin. Like a reptile."

"Like a spider?"

"Sure—like a spider. Or a snake. It's absolutely fascinating."

"It sounds painful," Rebecca said.

"That's one of the strange things. It isn't. Or, he claims it isn't. The patient. Underneath, he just has new skin. We have absolutely no idea what's causing it."

"Oh," Rebecca said. "Well."

"His council house is falling down. The foundations are built into very sandy soil—it's very biblical. And he's a drinker."

"I suppose I might be as well," Rebecca said, "in that situation."

"We never know if he's going to turn up to our appointments," Guy said, fake-exasperated. "And he stinks of alcohol. It's pretty grim."

Rebecca looked at Guy's skin, all pink and yellow and red in places.

"Sounds it," she said.

"Can I say something, Rebecca? You really do look beautiful today. Stunning." Some of Guy's spit landed on Rebecca's face again. "How's Julius? You're far too good for him," he said, then laughed, like he'd told a joke, but Rebecca could see that he meant it.

"Oh," Rebecca said. "My bus. Nice to see you, Guy."

"So nice," Guy said. "We must get coffee sometime. I see you at the staff canteen."

"Say hi next time," Rebecca said, and got on the bus. Though she didn't look out of the window, she could tell Guy was still standing at the bus stop, watching her pull away, possibly waving.

I stopped reading. I walked across the landing to the bathroom. The floor was damp and soft underneath me.

I was drunk but felt not.

I took off all my clothes.

I tried to pick at my skin. I picked at my chest first, right at the edge of the new part.

But I couldn't lift any of the skin from my chest. Or from my left hand, where it had come off, either.

It just hurt really bad.

I sat down on the edge of the bath and bent double and looked at the skin on my dick and around my thighs. I could still see the ridges on my thighs where the old skin was raised over the new skin.

I forced my long and blue thumbnail underneath the old skin.

Some of me came away. I began to bleed into the bath. The sound of it on the porcelain.

I pushed my nail in deeper.

I used the nail of my thumb to pull the skin upward. More blood came out.

I levered my hand upward, pulling the skin with my thumb like a fishhook.

The blood started coming faster. Like there was an important artery there.

It ran down my leg and dropped and then pooled in the valley area of the expensive bathtub. The pool got bigger. Once it was pooled it started moving toward the plughole.

There was a big hole now. In my thigh. The size of the end of my thumb.

But no skin was coming loose.

I took the showerhead and turned it on and put cold water onto the hole. I felt the muscles around it contract. Like a dead thing electroshocked.

I tried to use the cold water and my thumb at the same time to pull the ridge of skin up. My thumbnail just slid deeper into my thigh.

The blood cleared and I could see the raw flesh, all pink and meatlike underneath the parts of me that I had dug away.

That night I dreamed the house was full of people. A party downstairs, going out into the garden. Empty and half-empty bottles of yellow and pink wine. Ashtrays all over, full of smoke and pale gray ash.

People I recognized and people I didn't. My brother and his wife, out back, much younger, holding champagne flutes, laughing, bleeding into and out of each other. The deer-man stood at the back of the garden with the rusty shears. Children running, maybe my nephew. I could not see their faces.

The boy and girl from the video. The same age, laughing together. Their faces changing, their size changing. Growing older, then younger. Snippets of conversation like I was too drunk. I saw the big and thin Spanish or South American man far away. I looked around for my mother but could not see her anywhere. All the plants in the garden growing bigger, visibly, fractally, in spirals, beginning to obscure the light that came into the house. The house itself flaking and canted and sinking into something.

Standing very close to the deer-man, watching over his shoulder as he used the rusty shears to endlessly prune the growing dream plants.

My girlfriend inside, hair short like the new author photo that I did not recognize. Beautiful and leaned way back on the breakfast bar. Tilting her head backward, laughing, not seeing me. Drink in hand. I had no drink. My hands were empty. I wanted to talk to her. To say all the things I wanted to say. But I couldn't arrange them in my brain.

A burning smell. My legs went in a different direction, away from the party, upstairs.

My father there, on the landing, naked except for his bathrobe, floating, oscillating from four to ten feet away from me, and oscillating in size, too. I wanted to say something. But my mouth would still not work. So he just floated there, naked except for his bathrobe, blood pooling between his legs, underneath his floating and naked blue-veined feet.

Again, the smell of burning.

I woke up in the bath.

There was dry blood stained down my thighs and on the white porcelain. There were tissues in the bath too, blood-crusted. I'd put a towel under my head at some point as a pillow.

My skin felt so cold. So did my insides. There was an empty wine bottle beside me.

The bleeding had stopped.

I stood but fell slightly. I stood again.

My leg really hurt. It was all stiff, too. My dick hung short above it, so retracted it was almost at a right angle from my body. My balls were all up in me. There was dried blood in my pubic hair.

I put my hand on the sink to steady myself. Then I stepped out of the bathtub with my bad leg.

I felt out of breath. I could feel my heart pushing my chest.

I stood still for a bit until the room stopped moving.

I took the showerhead that had been lying between my legs and turned it on hot and blasted the bathtub. The dry blood lifted slowly from the porcelain and the water turned pink. Once it was mainly clean I stepped back into the bath and cleaned the hole in my leg. It stung and began to bleed again. But after a little while it stopped.

I knew I should eat but I wasn't hungry. So I went upstairs to check on the plants. I wanted to make sure they were doing okay.

I wanted to check the door to the second attic was closed, too.

I looked around to see if it felt like anyone was watching me. But I couldn't see anything. I couldn't feel anything, either.

The second attic door was closed properly, as I'd left it.

But underneath the door, coming from the second attic into the first, I saw new mold, black, pooling.

My father's bathrobe was still hung there on the back of the bedroom door.

The plants looked like teenagers. They were larger and just fine.

I felt proud of them just then.

Downstairs, I smoked and waited for my mother's care home to open.

I remembered something else from the night before. I was in a windowless basement restaurant, on a date with a girl who wasn't my girlfriend.

I wanted to impress the girl. I wanted to seem dangerous. So I told her I was a werewolf.

"Isn't it a full moon tonight?" she said.

I panicked. I thought: style it out, style it out.

"Yeah," I said, "and I have to go do werewolf stuff now."

I left the restaurant without paying.

Then the narrative of the dream changed into something I couldn't remember.

At the care home I sat in a blue plastic stackable chair. My mother sat in her usual disgusting chair.

"You're limping," my mother told me.

"Yeah," I said.

"I saw a deer from the window yesterday," she said. She pointed out of the window at the extremely busy road. "How are you? Are you eating? It's so lovely to see you."

"Yeah," I said. "Was there really a deer there? That's a road. A busy road."

"Your face looks bad, too," she said. "It's cut."

"I got in a fight. With the estate agent."

"You're selling the house," she said. "You should sell the house. The house must be worth a lot of money now. We paid off the whole mortgage."

"Your mother says we shouldn't sell it," I said. "She said estate agents are parasites. And I don't want to clear it out."

"Your grandmother is a Russian communist," my mother said. "A spy."

"She's from London," I said, "she's Scottish."

"A cunning backstory," my mother said, grinning. Then she looked out of the window at the road.

"Mum," I said, too loud.

"Or maybe it wasn't yesterday," she said.

"I was watching an old video," I said. "A home video."

"What?" my mother said.

"I found it in the attic. I should have taken pictures, to show you. You're in the video."

"I remember we had a video camera," my mother said. "Your brother loved it."

"He's in it. You're in it, too. So's Dad."

My mother looked down at her hands.

"But there's another family there, too," I said. "These children. And this man. I think his name is Julius." I was talking too fast.

"What?" my mother said.

"There's a car in it, too," I said. I tried to slow down without losing her attention. "It's the same car as in your manuscript, Mum. The one I told you about."

"Your manuscript?" my mother said.

"Your manuscript, Mum. The one I told you about. I found it in your study. Upstairs."

"There is no upstairs here. There's no study. This is a care home."

"At the house," I said, "not here."

"You're selling the house," my mother said.

"Mum," I said. She grinned.

"No upstairs here," she said. "Stairs and the elderly are mortal enemies."

"It's not funny. It is important."

"Gabriel," she said, "I'm sorry. I don't know what you're talking about. I don't remember a manuscript. Some days I think I don't even remember the day before."

She put her hand out and into mine. And then on top of it.

"Okay," I said.

"I'm sure everything's all right," my mother said. "Or if it isn't right now, I'm sure it will be in the morning."

"Okay, Mum," I said, "please tell me if you remember anything about it."

"It's a mystery," she said, in a television magician voice, smiling at me.

"Right," I said.

I don't know anything about these either," said my brother, on the phone. I had sent him photos of the video. "I don't know who those people are."

"It's weird, right? The car is in Mum's manuscript. And here in real life."

"It's not weird. It's just a video."

"She said she didn't know anything about it," I said.

"Your parents had lives before you were born."

"It's after. I think she's lying."

"She is a very sick woman. She is demented. She is not lying to you."

"I think she's lying," I said, again.

"Please," my brother said. "Please just clear out the fucking house. It is putting stuff in boxes. It is not that hard."

"My skin is all peeling off. That's in the manuscript, as well. In the second version. I'm frightened."

"Are you using the cream they gave you?" he said.

"No," I said, "I want a second opinion."

"You're ugly, too," my brother said. "How's that?"

But later my phone rang again. I heard my mother's voice say hello.

"Hello," she said.

"Hey, Mum," I said.

"I do remember the book," she said. "The book you were talking about today. I wanted to call before it goes again."

"What do you remember?"

"It's like you said," she said, "it's a book about a mother who dies. And she has a husband and two children. And she dies in the car of another man."

"That's how I read it the first time," I said. "Then it changed."

"The great sadness of it was going to be that the husband never knew why the mother character was in the car. He didn't know if his wife was being faithful when she died. But the reader knew she was. She had just accepted a lift. And the husband has to build a new life never knowing."

"Right," I said, "but there's another book there. When I read it again it had changed. She wasn't married to Guy, the husband. She was married to Julius, the man who gave her the lift. The children had a different father."

"I don't know anything about that," my mother said, "but maybe I remembered wrong."

"How does it end? Did you write the end?" I said.

"Maybe," my mother said, "I'm sorry. I don't remember. Maybe it's there. You should check."

"I will," I said. I took a drink from the bottle of wine I was holding. "Can you call me if you remember anything else?"

"I'll try," my mother said.

"Thanks, Mum," I said. "Love you."

"How are you? Are you eating?"

"I am eating," I said. "Thanks for asking."

After we got off the phone I went upstairs to my mother's study. I wanted to read more of the manuscript.

The room was dark but the curtains were open.

In the dark I was sure I saw movement at the window. I heard the sound of rusted metal on metal. Like feet on a ladder.

I went over to the curtains and closed them.

I looked at the black mold on the wall. It seemed bigger still. But maybe that was because it was dark. In it I sort of saw the pattern of a figure. A broken neck. Two bulbous eyes staring out at me, upside down.

I sat down at the desk and turned on the lamp. Transparent blue light filled the room. I looked at the mold. The figure was gone. But the mold seemed bigger, worse.

I turned to my mother's desk and started reading where I'd left off last.

But the pages were blank.

I kept turning them. And then I found something.

CHAPTER FIVE

✦

When Harry woke, the clock said three forty-three in the morning. He shifted slightly on the mattress and felt that around him, again, the sheets were soaked with his own sweat gone cold. The draft from the roof had gotten worse. It came as a strong light wind, full of dark outside. He swung his legs off the bed and felt rainwater on the cold floor under the new skin of his bare feet.

He dressed in all his yesterday clothes and looked down at his skinned hands. He wasn't so old but he felt it and his hands had seen so many things. Deep lines in them. He turned them over in themselves, looked at his palms. His heart line, intuition line, line of Mars. He took a drink from the bottle on the floor and felt it warm his throat, waited to see if the dream would leave him.

But it wouldn't. A train he was on, hurtling at hundreds of miles an hour toward the sea. Passing another train going in the same direction at almost the same speed. For a moment, both of them still, and through the windows seeing the passengers on the other train as if they were together and not moving at all. Catching the eye through the glass and the glass of another passenger, a much younger man, himself skinned like he was.

Then accelerating away. And getting off the train and swimming, across the sea, which he somehow knew was the Channel. To an island in it.

And how cold the petrol was on his new and old skin and the smell of it. And the sharpness of the metal of the cigarette lighter. It struggling to spark in the air that was full of water. And the black branches of the dying, gray tree above him against the night sky.

And then it sparking and how good it felt, how warm, the warmth of it. What was the word that the university doctor kept using? Exfoliate. A total exfoliation. And knowing that soon he would live in tree roots.

He was so tired. Of waking up in the cold sweat. Of finding that there was more of himself underneath him.

Leaving the house for the train station, Harry took a last look at his home. It was so leaning and broken. The walls all peeling away like himself, the broken glass, the missing roof parts. The cling-filmed windows. If they'd fixed it, maybe—

The train ticket took almost the last of his money. He huddled himself on a bench in the outside, waiting for the first train of the morning that would carry him to his sea, his island.

The narrative jumped ahead, skipping chapters. Blank pages between them. I kept reading.

✢

Guy took a long time to answer the door. Rebecca realized, standing there, waiting, that she was sweating slightly. It went cold quickly in the conditioned air. She was nervous. She'd never been to this part of the campus before.

She belonged in Humanities, really. It was cozier, more casual, full of shuffling women in men's cardigans and young female students quietly laughing and talking. Here, in the Sciences, staff and students walked purposefully and metallic equipment made strange and industrial noise.

Guy's skin was worse than when Rebecca had seen him last, at the bus stop. A couple of the sores on his face were actively leaking pus. He was sweating, too. It mixed with the pus and made his face shine horribly. He smiled broadly.

"Rebecca," he said, "a welcome surprise."

"Hello, Guy."

"Come in, come in. Sit down," he said. He was blocking the doorway. Rebecca stepped past him and sat down primly in the chair next to his desk.

Guy's office was disgusting. The wastepaper bin was full of sandwich containers from the canteen and fast-food packaging. The sandwich containers said things like "Egg Salad" and "Tuna Melt." There were four or five half-drunk cups of cold, milky tea lingering, along with energy-drink cans and cardboard soda cups. There was popcorn everywhere for some reason, littered between used and crumpled tissues and napkins. Open next to the crusted computer keyboard was a vat of slightly discolored E45 moisturizing cream. Rebecca noticed loose hairs half-submerged in it.

Guy sat down in his desk chair. It sagged underneath him noticeably.

"What can I help you with, Rebecca?" He tried to hold eye contact with her. Rebecca looked up and away.

"You mentioned something about a patient of yours. Or someone you're studying. A subject."

"Yes."

"You said all their skin was peeling off. Like a reptile."

"Yes," Guy said.

"Have you worked out what's causing it yet?"

"Well," Guy said, "no, not really. We have some working theories. But it's essentially a mystery. At this time."

"Is it harmful? Do you think they're in danger?"

"I—why are you so interested? You're shaking," Guy said. Rebecca looked down at her hands. She moved them into her lap.

"It's Felix," she said. She hadn't wanted to tell him. But she didn't seem to have another choice.

"Your son," Guy said.

"It started a few weeks ago. At first I thought it was just bad eczema. So I took him to a doctor. They gave him some hydrocortisone. But it hasn't stopped."

"No," Guy said.

"So I took Felix to a specialist. But they said the same thing: just childhood eczema. But his skin keeps coming off. In huge sheets."

"And underneath?"

"It's just the same. Just new skin. Just fresh skin."

"I see," Guy said.

"And I'm worried about him. He doesn't seem to realize that it's not normal. But he's acting strangely. He's quiet and withdrawn. He seems confused a lot of the time. More than Joanna. His sister. More than a normal child."

"I can understand why it would be confusing." Guy said, "Is he sleeping?"

"What? Not properly. He comes to us some nights. I don't know what to do."

"He's dreaming?"

"I think so. Why?"

"No reason," Guy said. "I can see why it would be confusing for him."

"So," Rebecca said, "I don't know what to do. I don't know who else to talk to. I hoped maybe you knew something."

Guy leaned forward in his chair. The plastic parts of it creaked.

"You seem very worried," he said.

"I am," Rebecca said. "How is your patient? The man with the same thing."

"Uh," Guy said. He leaned back again, swung around slightly so he wasn't looking at her. "I don't want to alarm you. It's probably completely unrelated. At least, it seems unrelated. He—Harry—he's missing. The police are involved, now."

Rebecca inhaled.

"I'm so sorry," she said.

"It's not—it could be completely unrelated."

"I don't understand," Rebecca said.

"He complained of these dreams. He wasn't sleeping. And his house was falling down. He believed that the house was somehow linked to his skin. That they were connected. But the council—he couldn't get it repaired."

"Jesus," Rebecca said.

"In the dream—he told me about it—he had to swim to this place. And there he could burn all of his old skin off. Just leaving the new skin. Like I said, it could be unrelated. Psychosomatic. He was a drinker. Quite mad."

"Felix's dream," Rebecca said.

"Well, yes," Guy said, "that's what concerns me. The problem is—without him here, I can't continue my tests. So I don't know much more than when we last spoke."

"You don't know anything? About the cause? Our house—we're moving. Or whether it's harmful?"

"Only a handful of theories," Guy said. "We really know very little about the skin. It's the largest organ of the body. We live in it. But we know so little about it, really. We can hide our blemishes, cut off the parts we don't like. But we have very little understanding of the things that cause the problems. In our skin."

Rebecca picked up her bag and placed it in her lap. She opened it and took out the transparent blue plastic sandwich bag with the sheets of Felix's skin inside. She had saved every one.

"Would this help?" she said.

"That's—"

"Felix," she said. "It's his. All of it that has come off. That I know about."

"May I?" Guy said. He reached toward her. Rebecca silently handed him the bag.

Guy took it and held it to the light.

"It's so clear," he said.

"Yes."

Guy opened the bag. He carefully inserted his index finger and thumb into it and pulled out one of the sheets of Felix.

Rebecca flinched.

Guy put the bag down on the desk and unfurled the piece of skin. Rebecca recognized it as being Felix's left hand. The second piece that had come loose.

Guy lifted it to his face, very close, and looked at it from behind his thick glasses. Rebecca heard him inhale deeply.

"I can work with this," he said. "I can work with this."

"All right," Rebecca said.

"Can you leave it with me?" he said, then inhaled deeply again.

Rebecca found herself nodding.

"Yes," she said. "Of course."

I stood and turned off the lamp.

I left the manuscript open.

I walked out of my mother's study. The hard floor felt soft underneath my feet. Like an inflatable deflating.

My leg really hurt now where I'd dug into it with my thumb.

I had to sit in certain positions on chairs. And it hurt to walk, too.

I felt scared. Of my leg and of the manuscript.

My mother had said that it was a different story. That it was the story of a woman who dies in the car of a man who isn't her husband. And the husband has to live not knowing why she was in the car.

This was not that story. It was different. But it had the same characters. And it'd had the same beginning. But then I reread it and it had changed.

I didn't know why it had changed. And I did not know why the skins were peeling off in the manuscript. Just like mine was.

And why the man's house was so fucked. And why mine was, too.

I wanted to look at my leg. So I went into the bathroom.

On the landing I could feel something watching me. The

light was on. So I couldn't see anything that was outside the landing window. The glass was just blue-black, reflecting all the indoors.

I pulled down the blue jeans I was wearing. I sat on the edge of the bath.

The hole in my leg was infected. I thought I had cleaned it properly. But maybe I hadn't. Or maybe it had just got infected anyway.

There was still a big hole the size and shape of my thumb.

It was red in the middle. Then up the edges of the hole it was yellow and damp with pus. A little green. The skin around it was yellow too, then red-pink. I touched it right in the middle. It hurt.

I undressed fully and stepped into the bathtub. I took the showerhead and set it on low but warm. I aimed it at the wound. It stung. Some of the pus and dried blood washed away. But mainly it stayed the same colors.

That night I was in a windowless basement restaurant, on a date with a girl who was not my girlfriend.

The girl ordered the Soup du Jour.

She tried it. Then she spat it out. She called the waiter over.

"I don't know what trick you're trying to pull," she said, "but I've had Soup du Jour before, and this ain't it."

"Hurrrrgggggnnhhhh," I said, flopping my massive whale flippers all over the table, knocking wine and water glasses to the floor. "Weeeooooooooow clik. Clk clk hrrrnnnggg."

I was in a waiting room, in a plastic and stackable chair. There were old women in other plastic chairs. There was a table with magazines. There was a man, standing, talking to a receptionist. The television on the wall said: *this has been in my family for a long time, but I'd be willing to part with it if the price is right.*

"What do you mean?" the man at the desk said, to the receptionist.

"Please don't raise your voice, sir," the receptionist said.

"You used to. You used to just fill these out."

"Sir," said the receptionist.

The man hit his hand on the reception desk. One of the sat-down old women jumped. Then the man made a gak sound and put his hand on his chest, where I assumed his heart was.

Then he fell on the floor.

The receptionist said, "Sir?"

The man rolled backward so he was on his side, facing me. He still had his hand on his chest. His body started spasming.

Then he closed his eyes and stopped.

Then he opened both his eyes and winked at me. So I grinned at him. Then he closed his eyes again.

"Sir?" said the receptionist.

She kept the same face on her face.

She picked up the phone on her desk and said something I didn't hear.

A doctor came out of the hidden doctor area. She knelt down beside the man. She checked if he was breathing then his pulse. Then she began to perform some kind of violent-seeming resuscitation technique.

The receptionist was out from behind the desk now.

"Don't hurt him," I said. She ignored me. Then she stopped.

"He's gone," she said.

"What?" I said. "No, he's not."

"You called the paramedics?" she said, to the receptionist.

"They're a minute or two away," the receptionist said.

"He's not dead. He's pretending," I said. They ignored me.

I stood outside and smoked while watching the man—now zipped into a specialist dead person blanket—being loaded into the ambulance.

It drove away, silent.

One of the old women turned to me as we began to file back into the waiting room.

"Why did you say that?" she said. "It wasn't funny. It was just disgusting."

I felt embarrassed. I didn't want to talk to the doctor anymore.

So I didn't say anything. I just limped away from the doctor's, back in the direction of the house.

At the front door, unlocking it, I noticed that more roof tiles had fallen to the gravel.

The tiles were all shattered.

The walls were peeling away from themselves.

I told my grandmother the story about the man.

"I thought he was pretending," I said, "because of what my brother said."

"Do you think he was actually dead?" she said. We were sitting in her living room. It was raining.

"The ambulance people said so. So did the doctor. They put a sheet on him."

"But he winked at you," she said.

"Yeah," I said.

"It sounds to me like he was still alive," my grandmother said, "and just pretending really well."

I said, "Beats moi."

We sat for a little while without talking, listening to the rain.

"Do you believe in ghosts?" I said.

"Yes," she said.

"Me too, I think," I said.

"I think—" she said, then stopped.

"What?"

"There are lots of universes. There are all the universes, with all the possibilities in them. And humans can imagine all of those universes."

"Yeah," I said.

"That's what I think ghosts are," she said.

We sat in silence for a while again. Her cat was on the windowsill, watching the rain. It was coming down harder now. My grandmother had finished her coffee. I didn't touch mine.

Slowly I watched her fall asleep.

Once she was, I stood and carried the two coffee cups to the kitchen and drained them and rinsed them and put them into her dishwasher. The cat had followed me into the kitchen. I put some biscuits into its bowl for it. Then I stroked it as it ate the biscuits.

My grandmother's study was upstairs. So was her bedroom. She could still sleep upstairs because she could still walk up stairs.

When the cat was done eating I went upstairs to see if I could fix the bed that my grandmother had been complaining about. She had said that it had been sliding across the floor in the night. There was probably something wrong with one of the legs or something.

The cat followed me upstairs.

I could not see anything wrong with the bed. It was sturdy to the touch. I lifted it and jiggled each leg and they were all firm.

I didn't really know what I would do if I found something wrong, anyway.

There were huge piles of books on either side of the bed. The bedspread was covered in pictures of scarlet macaw parrots flying. Or sitting down on branches. It smelled good. When I stopped moving the bed, the cat jumped up on it and walked around and then sat down. I sat beside it for a while, stroking it until it fell asleep.

I stood and walked quietly into my grandmother's study. I didn't want to wake the cat or my grandmother. There were even bigger piles of books in the study, leaning against bookcases that went all up the walls. There was a desk with a very old computer and a printer, and behind it a big window that looked onto the garden that made the room bright. It was very quiet except for the rain. There was a thick wad of paper on the desk.

I sat down in the chair in front of the desk and looked out of the window for a while. Then I looked down at the manuscript. The title said: *Fables / Aphorisms: A Memoir.* I turned to a random page.

This is a true story: Tsutomu Yamaguchi worked for Mitsubishi. He was a businessman. He was on a business trip. He was on a business trip to Hiroshima. He had been on the business trip for three months, and this was the last day of the business trip. So Tsutomu Yamaguchi was walking with his two colleagues—Akira Iwanaga and Kuniyoshi Sato—to the train station, to go back home.

But Tsutomu Yamaguchi realized that he had left his travel papers at work.

So, alone, he walked back. He could not travel without the papers.

When he was by the docks he saw a plane fly overhead. Then he saw two small parachutes.

Then he saw a flash in the sky.

Then the flash in the sky knocked him clean off his feet.

The eardrums of Tsutomu Yamaguchi exploded. And his skin was burned all over. He crawled to a shelter where he rested a night. Then he went out to find his work colleagues, Akira Iwanaga and Kuniyoshi Sato. They had survived the bombing, too.

So they all three returned home, to Nagasaki. There he was treated for his burns. And the day after, Tsutomu Yamaguchi went back to work.

And—at eleven in the morning—when the same bright flash happened in the sky, and knocked him off his feet, all Tsutomu Yamaguchi could think was: again? Again?

This is a true story: on a farm lived a pig. In the pen next to the pig lived a scarlet macaw parrot.

The farmer fed the pig every day from a big pile of the most delicious barley. It was the best barley on the farm. The pig boasted to the parrot that it must be the most-loved animal, because it got to eat the best barley.

"The farmer must love me very much," said the pig. "Certainly the farmer loves me more than you."

"That does seem to be the case," said the parrot, sadly.

The pig ate so much of the delicious barley that it got fat. But still it boasted.

"I am very fat, and very, very loved," said the pig. "You are thin, and loved less."

"That does seem to be the case," said the parrot, sadly.

One day, when the pig had eaten half of all of the delicious barley, the farmer came to the pigpen with shears. The pig was too fat to move. The farmer chopped off the pig's head with the shears.

Then the farmer took the pig to the market to be sold and eaten.

The next day, seeing that there was plenty of delicious barley left, the farmer brought some to the parrot.

But the parrot refused to eat it.

"Why do you refuse to eat the delicious barley?" said the farmer.

"Because," said the parrot, "I know that if I eat the delicious barley, it will make me fat, and then you will cut off my head."

"What a clever parrot you are," said the increasingly fat farmer, his mouth full to the brim with the nearly irresistible barley.

FABLE 21

+

This is a true story: when the bomb hit at the school, children were cooked as if microwaved.

They stayed alive because their insides were alive. But their skin boiled on their faces, began to melt off.

Their faces and their forearms, too. Their little legs.

So the schoolteacher—her skin also melting—took the classroom scissors and went to their throats one by one.

I put the manuscript back together. She was meant to be writing a memoir. This didn't seem like a memoir. But it didn't seem to matter.

I went back to check on the cat. It was still asleep on the bed. I sat down beside it. Then I gnashed my teeth at it like I was going to bite its head off. As if the cat were the pig from the fable, or John the Baptist.

Then I kissed it on its sleeping head.

Downstairs my grandmother was still sleeping, too. I went to the kitchen and made her a glass of water. Then I carried it back to where she was sleeping and put it down beside her. And then I let myself out of the front door, locking it behind me.

Sometimes I wondered when would be the last time I did that.

I limped back to the house. It was still raining but I had sunglasses on. My hair was all wet. I slicked it back like a movie Italian.

In my grandmother's favorite field, I saw a small woman deer, chomping excess foliage.

I stood there for a while in the rain looking at it.

It did not look frightening. It looked small. And far away. And like it was meant to be there.

A car passed. The deer deer-ran away, out of its field and into dense trees.

I heard the passing car stop, then reverse back to me. I turned around. It was the metallic-blue car. The one the boy and girl drove around.

The window went down.

"Why are you standing in the rain?" the girl said.

"I'm looking at this deer," I said.

"I don't see a deer," the girl said.

"They're very sneaky," I said.

"Want a ride?"

"I thought you were cross with me," I said.

"You can't stand there in the rain. Looking at an imaginary deer."

"Where are you going?" I said.

The girl looked over at the boy.

"We're going to drive into the ocean," he said.

"Sure," I said. "Can you run down that deer first?"

I rode in the back seat. The boy and the girl sat up front. I did finger guns at the deer field as we drove away from it. The rain on the soft top of the car was making a good sound. My wet clothes were making the tan leather seats dark.

We took the bridge over the estuary, past the strange birds and electricity pylons that lived there. The bad neighborhoods at the edge of the town. A roundabout with drive-through restaurants and a bowling alley. Then we drove through the forest, to the ocean. The infected hole in my leg hurt through my saturated jeans.

They stopped the car in a car park that faced the ocean. The boy leaned back and opened his hand at me. Inside his hand was a blue circular pill. I took it without saying anything. I crunched it up in my teeth.

I said, "Thanks, Felix."

"That's not my name," he said, "that's a cat name."

"And I suppose yours isn't Joanna," I said, to the girl. She didn't say anything. We sat listening to the rain for a moment.

"How'd you fuck your face up this time?" Felix said, through the rearview mirror.

"I got in a fight. With an estate agent."

"You're selling the house?" the girl said.

"You need to not do that," Felix said.

"I don't want to," I said.

"I'm serious," Felix said, "like really fucking serious."

"You need to take better care of it," the girl said. "It's important."

"Right," I said.

Then I said, "Hey, Felix, did all your skin ever peel off?"

"All my skin?" he said.

"Yeah. Like a reptile."

"Uh," he said, "no."

"You sure?"

"Yeah."

"Maybe when you were a child? And you were too young to remember."

"Maybe that happened to me."

"You can't remember now. Because you were a child."

"Maybe," he said.

The wind was picking up and making the rain come sideways. The blue-gray sea was so full of movement you couldn't even see the rain land.

I closed my eyes and listened to the sound of it.

I woke up back at the house. My stomach hurt but my leg hurt more. I didn't remember driving away from the ocean, or coming back to the house.

I wondered what the pill was.

When I went downstairs, the front door was closed and the car was not outside. I made myself a glass of water from the tap. It was dark out. The kitchen clock said 03:43. I didn't know if that was right.

I went upstairs again to the bathroom to look at my leg. It hurt really bad now. It took me a long time to do the stairs. There was a strong draft coming from somewhere cold, full of black outside. I shivered in it.

In the bathroom I rolled my wet jeans down. I had slept in them. The muscles, even in my good leg, were tight. I must have been in the rain recently. It was still raining outside. I could hear it.

The hole was still extremely infected. Maybe worse. It was pink in the middle of it, with a yellow ring, but now there was even more green around it, too. The more green seemed bad. I took off the rest of my clothes and stepped into the shower. I turned it on hot.

It was cold at first, which made my muscles electroshock a little. Then it warmed up. I stood there for a while, just letting the water warm the veins that went up my neck. It felt good. I let my hair get wet, too. My eyes were closed.

But I opened them and looked back down at the hole in my leg. I moved how I was standing so the shower water hit it right. It hurt bad when I did that.

I stepped out of the water. I looked down at the hole. I noticed that the skin was lifting around it slightly.

I put my thumbnail under the rift. The skin came away easily. The infected skin. I pulled it up and away from my thigh. The light through the infected skin-flap made it translucent pink and yellow and green.

The skin underneath was fresh and uninfected.

I kept pulling.

I pulled the skin from where the hole was. It all came away. The green ring and the yellow ring and the pink eye of it.

All of it came away from my thigh. And it kept coming, all down my leg, right down the side of my shin.

Once I had all that would come in my hand, I tore it away, like a wet paper napkin.

I looked at it in the bathroom light.

There was a little pus and blood. But when I checked my actual leg there was none there.

The dead skin in my hand was horrible.

I dropped it on top of the plughole and let the water from the shower disintegrate it.

All the colors of it made it look like plant matter in a quickly moving river after a storm.

I washed the new skin on my leg. It was perfect, almost hairless, uninfected. There was a pockmark where the wound had been. Like a big acne scar.

I dried myself and walked to my bedroom.

My leg didn't hurt now.

On my phone there was a missed call from a number I didn't recognize. But I didn't call it back.

When I woke up again it was light. I found two of my girl-friend's old T-shirts in a wardrobe. She must have left them when visiting a long time ago. One was white, and said RUS-SIAN ASSETS in black across the top of the chest. The other was blue and said BRAT. It smelled of her, just about. Or I hoped it did.

The kitchen smelled really bad, of stale alcohol and stale smoke, and the black-mold smell, the fungus smell. I used a dirty Le Creuset espresso cup for the coffee. It looked better than the other options.

I heard the television from the other room. It was singing in an old-timey voice. It sung: *you might think you left me all alone. But I can hear you talk without a telephone.*

Except for that the whole house felt quiet. But I felt like I was not alone. My neck hurt when I turned to look around either side of me.

I took my coffee to my father's study. It was on the ground floor. I had not been in there, really. Not since the estate agent had told me that it could be a bedroom.

It was dark because the curtains were closed. There were piles of papers and an empty ashtray on the huge dark-wood desk. It didn't seem like it would be a good bedroom. It was too dark. And it was on the wrong floor for bedrooms to be on.

The papers were handwritten in horrible, cheap spiral-bound notebooks. There were biros everywhere, incomplete and complete crosswords, old betting slips. Dead cigarette butts and roaches in ashtrays.

I touched the end of one and it was so dry.

I took one of the notebooks at random and turned to the first page. The handwriting was hard to read. But I could read it because I recognized it so well.

THE TAPE

INT. UNIVERSITY CORRIDOR, DAY

It's the 1980s. ROBIN, a bookish girl, is picking her
possessions off the floor. All the students are in
80s clothes: big hair, eyeliner, shoulder pads. Blue
denim on the boys. Other students are around, half
watching, going into classrooms. ELIZABETH bends
down to help her.

> **ELIZABETH**
>
> Oh my God, I'm so sorry. I didn't mean to
> push you.

> **ROBIN**
> (picking up books)
>
> That's all right.

> **ELIZABETH**
>
> You're so pretty. I haven't seen you before.

> **ROBIN**
>
> I just transferred. Mid-semester. My dad—

> **ELIZABETH**
>
> Cool, that's great. My name's Elizabeth.

                    ROBIN

   I'm Robin.

                  ELIZABETH

   Isn't that a boy's name?

                    ROBIN

   It can be a girl's name.

They walk together into one of the classrooms.

INT. LECTURE THEATER, DAY

A LECTURER is shuffling papers at the front of the
class. The room is half-occupied. A hushed murmur.

                  ELIZABETH

   Come sit with me?

                    ROBIN

   Sure. Thanks.

Elizabeth sits close to the front. She folds down
the seat next to her for Robin and pats it. Robin
sits.

The lecture begins. Extremely boring. The lecturer
might as well be talking like one of the adults in
Peanuts. Minutes pass.

LECTURER

The general k-Fibonacci sequence was found
by studying the recursive application of
two geometrical transformations used in the
well-known 4-triangle longest-edge (4TLE)
partition. This sequence generalizes,
between others, both the classical
Fibonacci sequence and the Pell sequence—

Elizabeth takes extremely neat, multicolored notes.
Robin notices. She has nothing written down.

The door to the lecture theater opens and PHIL
enters. He is handsome, boyish, well-built.

PHIL
(to the lecturer, silently)

Sorry.

Phil sits beside Robin, who is sitting beside Elizabeth. Elizabeth leans over to him.

ELIZABETH
(whispering)

Hey.

Phil shushes her, then grins. Elizabeth laughs. He
turns to Robin.

PHIL
(whispering)

I'm Phil.

INT. ROBIN'S HOME, NIGHT

Robin sets a plate of mashed potatoes, sausages, and peas onto her FATHER's lap. He is clearly very sick. The television is on in the background. Some 80s show.

He begins to cough. Robin passes him a tissue.

He stops coughing.

> FATHER
>
> Your first day.

> ROBIN
>
> It was interesting. I met some interesting people.

> FATHER
>
> The lecture? What was it on?

> ROBIN
>
> Um, Fibonacci.

> FATHER
>
> Hmm.

He attempts to eat some peas. They mainly fall off his fork.

> ROBIN
>
> I'm going out tonight. With the people I met.

FATHER

Good. Making friends is good.

ROBIN

Yeah.

INT. ROBIN'S BEDROOM, NIGHT

It's a teenage girl's bedroom. Robin looks out of
place. She has changed clothes: into jeans and a
jumper and a jacket. Boy clothes.

EXT. SUBURBIA, NIGHT

It's winter. Robin walks through a suburban student
neighborhood. Other students are moving between
parties, holding blue and black plastic bags full of
cans of beer and bottles of cheap wine.

EXT. PHIL'S HOUSE, NIGHT

A student house. A mattress in the overgrown front
garden, an overflowing bin. Music coming from
inside. Robin knocks on the door. She waits.
ALEX answers. He has long hair, is skinny, eczema
covering his face and hands.

ALEX

Password?

ROBIN

Um.

ALEX

I need the password.

ROBIN

I don't have it. Phil invited me.

Alex rolls his eyes, closes the door almost all the
way, turns back toward the inside.

ALEX
(shouting)

Phil?

ALEX
(faux-apologetic)

We have a very strict door policy.

Phil appears at the door, puts an arm around Alex.

PHIL

Did I not tell you the password?

ALEX

She doesn't have the password.

ROBIN

You didn't tell me it.

PHIL

We'll let you off this time. Come in. We're
about to put the tape on.

INT. PHIL'S LIVING ROOM, NIGHT

The room is full of cannabis smoke. Elizabeth is there, and a stocky, nondescript boy with bruising on his face—MAX.

ELIZABETH
(hugging Robin)

You came!

Robin stays standing awkwardly. Phil kisses Elizabeth on the mouth.

PHIL

This is Alex. That's Max.

MAX

Hi.

ROBIN

What happened to your face?

MAX
(pointing at his face)

This? You should have seen the other guy.

ROBIN

What's "the tape"?

ALEX

The Best Years of Our Lives.

ROBIN

The old sitcom?

PHIL

Sit down.

Robin sits.

ROBIN

You get together on a Friday night to watch a sitcom from ten years ago?

ALEX

Do you have a problem with that?

ROBIN

No.

Max passes Robin a joint. She inhales.

ELIZABETH

Do you have the notes?

ALEX
(pulling thick, heavily used notepad
from back pocket, sitting)

I've got them, I've got them.

ELIZABETH

Turn the music off.

Phil turns the music off, sits beside Robin.

                    MAX
        (standing, turning on television and VCR)

    Let's go.

The television flickers gray and white. Then the
tape starts. A 70s British sitcom theme song.

                    ALEX

    OK, it's started, it's beginning.

                    MAX

    Usual theme song, no change.

Alex takes a note.

On the television, a title card appears: *THE BEST
YEARS OF OUR LIVES*. Then freeze frames of the main
characters laughing, with their actor credits: John
Hutchinson as DAVEY. Charlotte Brown as MOLLY. Dominic
Falvey as SPIKE.

                  ELIZABETH

    Usual intro sequence, no change.

Alex takes a note.

                    ALEX

    Yep, yep.

INT. CAFE, DAY

On the television. Molly is wiping down the cafe
counter. Spike is leaning against the counter. She
is short and buxom, he is tall and thin. Theme music
playing, Molly and Spike chatting inaudibly. The
theme music ends.

Davey bursts through the door. He is short and
stocky, wearing a coat, gloves, a scarf, and a hat.

INT. PHIL'S LIVING ROOM, NIGHT

ELIZABETH

Look, it's snowing!

PHIL

Is it? He's just wearing winter clothes.

MAX

That's a change.

ALEX

Yep.

Alex notes this down. Phil jumps off the sofa and
gets very close to the television.

ELIZABETH

Look at the window.

                              ALEX

Don't block it.

                              PHIL
                            (grinning)

She's right.

                            ELIZABETH

I told you.

                              PHIL

It's snowing, out the window. You can
barely see.

                              ALEX

Wait for the exterior scene, outside the
house. We'll be able to see properly then.

INT. CAFE, DAY

                              DAVEY
                            (proudly)

Well, I'm going to buy it.

                              MOLLY

You what?

                              DAVEY

The old Smith house. I'm buying it.

SPIKE

But Davey—

MOLLY

You're buying it? You ain't got no money.

DAVEY

Yes, I do, but that doesn't matter.

SPIKE
(scared)

But Davey—it's haunted. I don't want to
live in a haunted house.

There is canned laughter.

SPIKE

Ghosties.

More laughter.

DAVEY

They're just old stories. And I'm getting
an excellent deal.

MOLLY

I'm not so sure they're just stories.
Besides, that place is a wreck. What are
you getting it for?

                    DAVEY

     Free.

Molly drops a glass on the floor. It crashes. Spike
starts, comically.

                    MOLLY
             (slaps hands on counter)

     Free?

INT. PHIL'S LIVING ROOM, NIGHT

                    PHIL

     No changes to this conversation.

                    ALEX

     Noted.

INT. CAFE, DAY

Davey walks up to Spike and pats him on the chest.

                    DAVEY

     On the proviso—(beat) that we spend one
     night there. Alone.

Spike faints comically. Molly rushes over to him and
fans his face with a napkin. Davey put his hands on
his hips, looks exasperated. Canned laughter and
applause. FADE TO BLACK.

INT. PHIL'S LIVING ROOM, NIGHT

Phil gets up and pauses the tape.

                    MAX

    Have we ever had a weather change?

                    ALEX
                (looking at notebook)

    No. This is unprecedented.

Max lights a joint, inhales, passes it.

                    ROBIN

    I don't understand.

                    ALEX

    Understand what?

                    ROBIN

    Are there lots of episodes on this tape?
    What changes are you talking about?

                    PHIL

    Just one episode.

                    ROBIN

    Then what are you checking? What changes?

ELIZABETH

Each time we watch it something in the episode changes.

ROBIN

What?

PHIL

The tape. On the tape. It's the same tape. The same episode. Only one episode on the tape. But somehow, every time we watch it, there's something different about it. It changes.

ROBIN

That doesn't make sense.

ALEX

It could be something as subtle as a line of dialogue being different. But sometimes whole characters have different actors. Or the set is different. Or a character will have a limp that they didn't have before.

MAX

Once, Spike was in a deer costume. For the entire episode. And none of the other characters referenced it at all.

ROBIN

Is this a joke?

PHIL

No.

ELIZABETH

She doesn't know that. Maybe we're playing
a joke on her.

ALEX

It's not a joke.

PHIL

It's not a joke. Come back next week.
You'll see.

ROBIN

You do this every week?

PHIL

Every Friday. Alex takes notes. To track
changes.

ALEX

There has to be a pattern.

ROBIN

This is insane.

INT. PHIL'S BATHROOM, NIGHT

Robin washes her hands, then stares at herself in the mirror. She is stoned.

INT. PHIL'S CORRIDOR, NIGHT

Robin exits the bathroom. Elizabeth is waiting.

                    ELIZABETH

    We left it paused for you.

                      ROBIN

    Thanks.

                    ELIZABETH

    What do you think of Phil?

                      ROBIN

    Phil seems nice.

                    ELIZABETH

    You know he's my boyfriend.

                      ROBIN

    I assumed.

                    ELIZABETH

    He's nice, isn't he?

ROBIN

Yes, he seems nice.

A pause.

ELIZABETH

You look tired.

ROBIN

I'm really stoned.

They laugh. Elizabeth steps past her, into the bathroom.

INT. PHIL'S LIVING ROOM, NIGHT

Robin enters. Phil starts the tape again. Elizabeth is still in the bathroom. Phil and Robin sit together. Phil passes her the joint. She inhales.

ROBIN

We should wait for Elizabeth.

Nobody says anything.

I stopped reading the script. I stood up and walked around the room for a bit. There were so many notebooks. I flipped through a couple.

They were all prose or scripts. Mainly television shows he wrote for or consulted on. But some for imaginary shows. I looked at them for a moment.

I went to the kitchen to get some wine. But there was none in the fridge. So I took a warm one from the rack. Then I put some of the racked bottles into the fridge.

I took the warm bottle back to the study and spiraled the cap off it. The script was still there. I was worried it would have disappeared. Or changed.

I looked backward at a few pages.

They were the same. I had remembered them all right.

I kept reading.

In the script, the television episode continued. It followed a familiar trajectory: Davey eventually convinced Spike to spend a night in the house with him. Molly quietly and firmly warned them that the stories might, in fact, be true. Davey was headstrong and cocksure in the face of the potential ghosts. People in the room—Alex, Phil, Elizabeth, mainly— kept murmuring "no changes." Alex took notes.

EXT. HAUNTED HOUSE, SUNSET

FADE IN. Davey and Spike are standing under a
lamppost, outside the gates of the haunted Smith
house. It is snowing. A tall, dark, KNOCK-OFF
CHRISTOPHER LEE character walks up to them.

INT. PHIL'S LIVING ROOM, NIGHT

> **PHIL**
> (smiling)

It's snowing.

> **MAX**

Look at that.

> **ALEX**

There's no need for snow in this scene.
It's shot on a soundstage.

> **ROBIN**

It's beautiful.

> **PHIL**

Yeah.

Robin and Phil make eye contact.

EXT. HAUNTED HOUSE, SUNSET

Knock-off Christopher Lee hands the keys to Davey.
He unlocks the gate, and he and Spike enter the
house to spend the night there.

I kept reading. The episode continued. The group of students watched mostly in silence, smiling, occasionally murmuring that nothing had changed. Davey and Spike attempted to spend the night in the house. Haunted things happened. Paintings eyeballed them around rooms. Doors closed and opened on their own. Things went bump. No changes.

Confused and frightened, Davey and Spike were separated. Spike hid in a wardrobe. Davey rushed into the room and moved the wardrobe in an attempt to barricade the door. Spike fell from the wardrobe draped in a sheet. Davey screamed at Spike, thinking he was a ghost. Spike screamed back at him. They ran out of the house together.

They slept in their car. They were woken up by Knock-off Christopher Lee tapping on the window. They startled, then rolled down the window. Christopher Lee said that because they didn't spend the night in the house they were not allowed to have it for free. Davey rolled the window up. He harshly admonished Spike for scaring them both from the house, which Davey insisted was not haunted. Spike apologized. Snow was falling in the morning light. There was a thick layer on the car.

EXT. SUBURBIA, NIGHT

Phil is walking Robin home.

> **ROBIN**
>
> Thanks for walking me home.

> **PHIL**
>
> I don't mind. I like the air.

> **ROBIN**
>
> I hope Elizabeth doesn't mind.

> **PHIL**
>
> Why would she? She was asleep.

Fewer students are around now. But still some, carrying the same blue and black bags of alcohol, drunker.

> **PHIL**
>
> Those look like snow clouds.

> **ROBIN**
>
> That would be good. If it snowed tonight.

> **PHIL**
>
> I think it will.

                    ROBIN

If it's a practical joke, it's a really
good one.

                    PHIL

What?

                    ROBIN

The tape. The whole thing. If it's a joke,
it's a good joke.

                    PHIL

You think it's a joke?

                    ROBIN

What you've told me is impossible. It's
insane.

                    PHIL
                 (grinning)

Yeah. It does seem insane.

                    ROBIN

Yeah.

                    PHIL

But it's not a joke. It's real.

ROBIN

Why didn't we watch it again right away?

PHIL

It doesn't work. Nothing changes. It stays the same each night.

ROBIN

Can I come back next week?

PHIL

Yeah. You're invited.

ROBIN

Thanks.

They walk some more.

PHIL

I don't know how it works. Or what it means.

ROBIN

Are there any theories?

PHIL

No good ones. Maybe—I don't know. Relativity. Some kind of link to other universes. Through the tape.

ROBIN

Right.

PHIL

Every choice they made while writing and
filming it. That would have made a new
parallel universe.

ROBIN

Maybe.

PHIL

The story is always the same. The story
hasn't changed yet. The basic parts. But
the things around it change.

ROBIN

The snow was really beautiful.

PHIL

Yeah.

They stop outside of Robin's house.

ROBIN

This is me.

PHIL

Nice place.

                    ROBIN

        Thanks.

Beat.

                    ROBIN

        Do you believe in them?

                    PHIL

        Ghosts?

                    ROBIN

        Parallel universes.

                    PHIL

        Uh. I think you choose a path between
        them, maybe.

                    ROBIN
              (stepping closer, slightly)

        What do you mean?

                    PHIL

        There's a universe where I kiss you right
        now. I could choose to live in that
        universe.

                    ROBIN

        That's a universe where Elizabeth is
        really pissed off. At me.

PHIL

At me, as well.

Phil leans forward and kisses Robin on the forehead.
He looks serious, then grins.

PHIL
(gesturing with his chin)

That universe, this universe.

ROBIN
(grinning)

This universe.

INT. ROBIN'S HOME, NIGHT

Robin's father is asleep in the chair she left him
in. She turns off the television and brings him a
glass of water. Then she silently goes upstairs to
bed.

I flicked through the next pages of the script. I wanted to get to the tape again. I wanted to know why it was changing, like the manuscript in my own house.

All week Robin thought about the tape and Phil. She spent the weekend studying at the public library, then the evenings with her father, cooking his dinner, washing up his plates, watching him fall asleep in front of the television. He didn't seem like he was very, very sick. Just tired.

Every lecture and every seminar she wanted Phil to be there. But also she desperately did not want him to be there. I could tell that from the script, even though it didn't say it.

I thought about the tape, too. Maybe it was a practical joke. But all the characters seemed so sincere, so well-rehearsed, so casual. It seemed impossible. But so did the extreme yearning Robin felt for Phil. So maybe it was possible that the tape changed with each viewing. Any of these things could be possible. Robin waited for Friday with her jumper around her knees. I kept reading.

EXT. PHIL'S HOUSE, NIGHT

Robin knocks. Alex answers. The eczema on his face
has cleared up.

                    ALEX

    Robin.

                    ROBIN

    I don't know the password. Your skin looks
    better.

                    ALEX

    I saw a doctor. There's no password. We
    made that up.

                    ROBIN

    You should have a password.

                    ALEX

    Yeah.

INT. PHIL'S LIVING ROOM, NIGHT

Phil and Elizabeth are curled up on one sofa. Max is
on the other, in the middle. Robin and Alex sit on
either side of him.

                    MAX

    Hey.

ROBIN

Hey.

ELIZABETH

Ready to believe us, Robin?

ROBIN

There could be two tapes. How come you
weren't in our lecture today?

Beat.

PHIL
(looking away)

We thought we'd skip it.

ELIZABETH

I drove us out to the forest. I have a
car. It's really beautiful out there.
Romantic.

ROBIN

Romantic.

ALEX

Let's start the tape. Last week was so
good.

Alex gets up, puts the tape in the machine, rewinds
it, presses play. Max passes Robin an open bottle of
red wine. She takes a long drink from it.

Freeze-frames of the characters laughing appear on the screen. Their credits appear below. John Hutchinson as Davey. Charlotte Brown as Molly. Dominic Falvey as Spike.

                         ALEX

    No changes.

INT. CAFE, DAY

On the television. Molly is wiping down the cafe counter. Spike is leaning against the counter. She is short and buxom, he is tall and thin. Theme music playing, Molly and Spike chatting inaudibly. The theme music ends.

Davey bursts through the door. He is short and stocky, wearing a cheap suit.

INT. PHIL'S LIVING ROOM, NIGHT

                         MAX

    Regular outfit, no coat.

                       ELIZABETH

    No snow this time.

                        ROBIN

    Jesus.

INT. CAFE, DAY

DAVEY
(proudly)

Well, I'm going to buy it.

MOLLY

You what?

DAVEY

The old Smith house. I'm buying it.

SPIKE

But Davey—

MOLLY

You're buying it? You ain't got no money.

DAVEY

Yes, I do, but that doesn't matter.

SPIKE
(scared)

But Davey—it's haunted. I don't want to
live in a haunted house.

There is canned laughter.

SPIKE

Ghosties.

More laughter.

DAVEY

They're just old stories. And I'm getting
an excellent deal.

MOLLY

I'm not so sure they're just stories.
Besides, that place is a wreck. What are
you getting it for?

DAVEY

Free.

Molly drops a glass on the floor. It crashes. Spike
starts, comically.

MOLLY
(slaps hands on counter)

Free?

Davey walks up to Spike and pats him on the chest.

DAVEY

On the proviso—(beat) that we spend one
night there. Alone.

Spike faints comically. Molly rushes over to him and
fans his face with a napkin. Davey put his hands on
his hips, looks exasperated. Canned laughter and
applause. FADE TO BLACK.

INT. PHIL'S LIVING ROOM, NIGHT

Alex stands and pauses the tape.

ALEX

No changes.

ROBIN

What? Of course there were changes.

ELIZABETH

Like what?

ROBIN

It wasn't snowing.

ALEX

Yeah. But the snow was atypical. The snow was a change. Not snowing is normal. Not snowing is not a change.

ROBIN

All right.

PHIL

Do you believe us now?

ROBIN

You could have switched the tapes.

ELIZABETH

It's the same tape.

                    ROBIN

I don't know that.

                    PHIL

I guess that's true.

                    ROBIN

It does seem more likely. But it's still
impossible.

                    ALEX

It isn't possible. That's why it's so
interesting.

Max leans, puts his arm around Robin, passes her the
bottle again. She lets him, takes a long drink from
the bottle.

                    ROBIN

I understand.

In the script, the tape continued. The storyline was the same. No changes. Alex was barely taking notes, just adding strikes into some complex and spiraling grid system that Robin guessed mapped out the episode. I flicked through the pages, looking for the next change.

EXT. HAUNTED HOUSE, SUNSET

FADE IN. Davey and Spike are standing under a lamp post, outside the gates of the haunted house. It is not snowing. Knock-off Christopher Lee walks up to them.

INT. PHIL'S LIVING ROOM, NIGHT

> **ROBIN**
>
> Something looks different.

> **Max**
> (punching Robin in the ribs)
>
> Yeah. It's not snowing.

> **ROBIN**
> (laughing)
>
> No. Something else.

> **PHIL**
>
> Robin's right.

Elizabeth breathes out audibly.

> **ALEX**
>
> No mustache.

> **MAX**
>
> What?

ALEX

Robin's right: no mustache.

ELIZABETH

Are you sure?

EXT. HAUNTED HOUSE, SUNSET

The camera cuts in to reveal Knock-off Christopher
Lee is totally clean shaven. He has a small piece of
tissue stuck to his face where he has cut himself
shaving.

INT. PHIL'S LIVING ROOM, NIGHT

ALEX

Look, pause it.

Phil jumps up and pauses the tape. The image judders
on-screen but is clear.

Alex stands, too. He points out the piece of tissue
on Knock-off Christopher Lee's face.

ROBIN

Wow.

PHIL

He cut himself shaving.

MAX

That's great.

                    ELIZABETH

    It's not snow.

                       PHIL

    It's something.

                       ALEX

    I'm always so frightened. That nothing will
    change.

                      ROBIN

    It's not as beautiful as the snow.

                       PHIL

    No, it's not as beautiful as the snow.

FADE TO BLACK.

INT. ROBIN'S HOME, NIGHT

Robin is alone in her living room. She stands by the
telephone for a long time, coils the cord around her
finger. Then she dials a number.

                      ROBIN

    Hello.

                       PHIL

    Robin?

                    ROBIN

Yeah.

                    PHIL

What's up?

                    ROBIN

Nothing. I can't stop thinking about the
tape.

                    PHIL

Yeah. I can't ever stop thinking about it.

                    ROBIN

The tape.

                    PHIL

Yeah.

                    ROBIN

I need to see it.

                    PHIL

Friday.

                    ROBIN

I need it now.

                            PHIL

The tape?

                            ROBIN

That's what I said.

                            PHIL

We watch on Fridays. We never don't watch
on Fridays.

                            ROBIN

It feels like it didn't happen. Or it
happened in another universe. All of it.
Us.

                            PHIL

Us.

                            ROBIN

Tell me it's real.

                            PHIL

The tape?

                            ROBIN

All of it. Is anyone else there?

                            PHIL

No. I'm alone.

                              ROBIN

        Let me come over. Please.

EXT. PHIL'S HOUSE, NIGHT

Robin knocks on the door, waits. Phil opens it.

                              PHIL

        Hi.

                              ROBIN

        Hi. Do you have it?

                              PHIL

        The tape?

                              ROBIN

        Yeah.

                              PHIL

        Yeah. It stays here. Do you want to come
        in?

                              ROBIN

        Yeah.

INT. PHIL'S LIVING ROOM, NIGHT

Phil and Robin are alone. They both have a mug of
red wine. The bottle is open. Phil is rolling a
joint. He is focused on that, not Robin.

                    ROBIN

Are you frightened?

                    PHIL

Do I seem frightened?

                    ROBIN

Yeah. A little.

                    PHIL

I feel like someone's watching me.

                    ROBIN

I don't want to break it. The tape.

                    PHIL

I'm frightened it will be the same.

                    ROBIN

The tape?

                    PHIL

I've never watched it like this.

                    ROBIN

Alone?

                    PHIL

I don't feel alone.

                    ROBIN

    We're alone.

                    PHIL

    I guess.

Robin stands. She goes over to the bookshelf, takes
the tape from it, takes it out of its sleeve.

                    ROBIN

    Is this it?

                    PHIL

    Yeah.

Robin turns on the television. She puts the tape
into the VCR. She presses play.

She goes and sits closer to Phil. He lights the
joint, then passes it to her.

VHS snowstorm appears on the television.

                    PHIL

    This is it.

The VHS snowstorm lasts a long time.

                    ROBIN

    What if it never happens?

                    PHIL

    Then it never happens.

The tape begins. Freeze-frames of the characters
laughing appear on-screen. Their credits appear
below. John Hutchinson as Davey. Charlotte Brown as
Molly. Dominic Falvey as Spike.

PHIL

OK, it's started, it's beginning.

The intro credits end. Then the VHS snowstorm
reappears.

ROBIN

What happened?

PHIL

I don't know.

ROBIN

God.

They sit waiting for a long time. Then the tape
restarts. Freeze-frames of the characters laughing
appear on-screen. Their credits appear below.

PHIL

It's started again.

ROBIN

Has that ever happened before?

PHIL

No, never.

The tape ends, goes back to snowstorm.

PHIL

Fuck.

ROBIN

I don't understand.

PHIL

We should be writing this down. This isn't
fair on the others.

ROBIN

I don't care.

The snowstorm continues. Robin puts her hand on
Phil's. He flinches but does not retract. Then the
intro credits roll again.

PHIL

Jesus.

When the intro ends again, and goes back to
snowstorm, Robin kisses Phil.

He initially resists, then kisses her back.

The intro credits roll again and again on the
television.

The script ended there. But there was one more page of notes.

ENDING???

Phil and Robin sleep together

Phil tells Elizabeth?

Elizabeth, driving, arguing with Phil, crashes

RIP Phil

Some beautiful scene at a service station, E in tears

Tape goes missing

The group blame Robin for Phil's death and the missing tape

Robin's father dies—she graduates alone

Yrs later Alex & Robin meet—OSTENSIBLY to catch up, really to ask each other abt the tape, where it is, etc. Neither know. They agree it was likely incinerated in the crash.

I felt drunk and drained. The bottle of wine was empty, too. There were other scripts in the notebook, and other notebooks on my father's desk. But it was cold in the study. And I didn't want to read anymore.

The ending written there was not satisfying. I wanted to know why the tape changed every time. Like the manuscript in my mother's study.

I went out of my father's study and took half of one of the pink Xanax bars and lay down on the sofa and waited for my thoughts to turn off.

Looking up at the ceiling, I saw new mold.

Eyes staring out of it upside down.

Vines growing in, from the outside, stems reaching through new cracks in the windows, the walls.

As I was falling asleep my phone rang. I did not recognize the number. It was not listed as a contact in my phone. It was someone's personal number. Not a landline. Or a business. So I picked it up.

I said, "Yeah?"

"Hey," my girlfriend's voice said.

"Hi," I said.

"Hi," she said.

I had not heard her voice in so long. Since before she left.

It sounded the same but deeper, the way girl voices can. Further away.

I tried to sound together.

"What can I help with?" I said.

Then I wished I hadn't said that.

"How are you?" she said.

"Uh, good," I said. "I read your story. In *Guernica*. About the oligarch and the paintings."

"That's good," she said.

"How are you?" I said.

"Where are you?" she said. "I tried to go to the flat. But you're not at the flat."

"I got rid of the flat. Don't you read your emails?"

"Right," she said.

"Where are you?"

"Uh," she said.

I heard voices laughing in the background.

"I got rid of the flat," I said. "I'm at my parents' home."

"Jesus," she said.

"Is there something you need? You took everything, I thought."

"I don't know. I'm drunk. I shouldn't have called."

"Me, too. It's nice to hear your voice."

"It's hard out here," she said.

"What?" I said.

"It's hard out here. I can't—nobody understands."

"I understood," I said.

I didn't really know what she was referring to.

"I just want to go home," she said.

"Me, too."

"I just want to be at home watching television on our sofa and eating our terrible chicken meal. And smoking on the balcony. And sleeping. And wearing your big jumper. That's all I want."

"Me, too. Why not?"

She stopped talking for a moment.

Then I heard her say something to someone else, in the room she was in.

It was loud where she was. The house felt so quiet, then.

"I was so unhappy," she said, into the phone.

"I was happy," I said.

"No, you weren't," she said.

"It was complicated."

"We were both so unhappy."

"And now?" I said.

"I shouldn't have called."

"You should come back," I said. "Please. I want to see you so much. All the time."

"I should not have called," she said.

"If you want it you can have it. You can have it all back. That won't ever change. I'm right here."

"Jesus," she said.

"What?"

"I shouldn't have called," she said, "I'm sorry."

"You can call."

"No," she said, "I can't, and I really shouldn't."

"Please," I said.

"I can't do all this over again."

"It's just nice to hear your voice," I said.

"Are you okay?" she said. "You sound fucked up."

"I'm not okay. All my skin is peeling off. And there's a video of my mother with a family I don't recognize."

There was a pause, filled with telephone noise, crowd noise, music.

"What?"

"And the family are in a manuscript Mum wrote, but doesn't remember writing. And I think two of the characters are here in real life, too. I've met them. A boy and a girl. But the manuscript changes sometimes. Once."

"Your skin is peeling off? That sounds like eczema."

"It's not eczema. It's in the manuscript, too. I'm very frightened."

"Moisturize. See a doctor."

"I did."

"And what did they say?"

"They gave me a cream."

"So use the cream," she said. "I have to go. I hope your skin gets better."

"All right," I said, and then stayed on the phone listening to nothing until she hung up.

The sound of the front door closing woke me up. I wasn't sure how long I'd slept. It was nighttime when I went to sleep and it was daytime now.

I was in my childhood bed. The last thing I remembered was falling asleep on the sofa. I did not know how I got upstairs.

I heard the voice of my brother and then my brother's wife. They set some luggage down. I heard my brother's wife go: Jesus Christ, Jesus Christ.

I put a T-shirt on that said TWO WORLD WARS AND ONE WORLD CUP.

I put some jeans on, too.

I went downstairs.

"You're alive," my brother said.

"Not everyone who lives here dies," I said.

"It looks like crackheads have broken in. And turned it into a crackhouse."

"This is a party house now. It's *Animal House*."

"I haven't seen that movie," my brother said.

I heard the downstairs bathroom flush. Then my brother's wife came out.

"Have you seen *Animal House*?" my brother said, to his wife. She looked around the room.

"I have now," she said.

She looked at me. Then she walked out of the room and carried one of the suitcases upstairs and then upstairs again.

"You're sleeping up there?" I said.

"In our parents' room?"

"Yeah," I said.

"Where else?" my brother said.

"You should be careful," I said, "I think it's haunted. Everyone who sleeps up there dies."

"Mum's not dead," my brother said.

"Not yet," I said.

"Shut up."

I went over to the fridge and opened it and got a beer for myself. I set it loudly down on the breakfast bar and opened it.

"Give me that," my brother said, so I did. Then I got another one for myself. He looked around the room.

"Is all this damp new?" he said. "I don't remember it being this fucked here."

I heard my brother's wife come back down the stairs.

"Why the fuck are you growing weed in the attic?" she said.

"What?" I said. "I'm not."

"Fuck's sake," my brother said.

"It was here when I got here."

"You are very clearly growing weed in the attic. There are plants. They are flowering. It stinks. There is a grow tent. There are elaborate fucking ultraviolet lights."

"Did you not see it when you slept there before?"

"At your dad's funeral? We didn't look in the attic."

"I'm surprised you didn't notice," I said.

"We had other things to think about," she said.

"It's Dad's," I said, "not mine."

"He was growing weed?" my brother said.

"Yeah."

"Cool. Is it good?"

"It's not ready yet. But the old stuff is dirt."

"It has been freshly watered," my brother's wife said. "The plants should be dead. You're a fucking idiot."

"I didn't want them to die," I said. "We could make some serious money."

"You said it's dirt," my brother said.

"It is illegal. You let us send an estate agent round to a place where you are growing cannabis. Which is illegal," his wife said.

"It was Dad's," I said.

"It won't make us any money if it's dirt," my brother said. He took a long drink from the beer then gave his wife a look.

"I thought it could help with the funeral costs," I said.

"The funeral costs that we paid?" my brother's wife said.

"Yeah. Those."

"I don't know why we thought you could do this. You are clearly incapable. You are almost thirty. And you can't even clear out a house. You've just made it worse."

"I'm not almost thirty," I said.

I was surprised when my brother and his wife immediately started clearing stuff and putting it into cardboard boxes that they had brought with them in their small and expensive car.

I wanted to say: you're starting already? But I didn't. I didn't want to make my brother's wife more cross. You can do the kitchen, Gabriel, she said. It's disgusting in there.

I heard them put the radio on in the other room, the room with the television in it. I thought about the photos and jewelry and the Xanax all piled up on the coffee table. And the tape in the VHS player.

I went into the room and watched them taking dusty books off the shelves for a moment. My eyes stung from it. I picked up the coffee table things and put them back into the shoebox and took the video from the player and put it into its tacky metallic-blue sleeve and put that into the shoebox too and carried all of it upstairs, to my mother's study, where it would be safe for now.

Downstairs, I heard the radio say: *number thirty-four on our list of fifty ways to love your liver.*

In the kitchen, I opened the door to the garden and left it that way.

I took a colander from one of the cupboards and put it down on the outside floor.

I went around the kitchen and took each of the ashtrays and things that had been used as ashtrays and emptied them into the colander, so that the colander caught the cigarette butts and roaches, and the blue-gray ash went through the holes in the colander and onto the ground.

There was a light and cold autumny breeze.

It caught a little ash each time.

The wind ash floated then disappeared like moments do.

I finished my beer and opened another.

When I was done the kitchen smelled bad but it was clean. My brother ordered terrible pizza and we ate it in there, my brother and his wife sitting at the breakfast bar, me standing or leaning against it.

"You look thin," said my brother's wife, to me.

"Thank you," I said.

"Have you been eating properly?"

"I've just lost a lot of skin."

"This pizza is terrible," my brother said. "And such large portions."

"How's the writing?" my brother's wife said.

"Perfect, excellent," I said. "I am excellent."

"How many words are you at? I heard you hadn't even started."

"Who told you that? Steve?" I said.

"You're retarded," my brother's wife said.

"Should doctors say retarded?" I said.

"Only doctors should say retarded. And retards. So you're allowed, too."

"So how long have you two been dating? How did you meet?" I said.

"We've been dating six weeks," my brother said. His wife

rolled her eyes. "We met at a support group for people with retarded brothers."

"I don't have a brother," said my brother's wife.

"And retarded brother-in-laws," my brother said.

"So you've been married before?" I said.

"Three times."

"Each," my brother said.

"It must be quite a change," I said, to my brother.

"Why's that?"

"Going from being married to three men to being married to a woman. They were men before. Because you're gay."

"You must be confused," my brother said, "on account of your retardation."

"No, I'm quite certain."

"Certainly retarded."

"Are you his beard?" I said, to my brother's wife. "Do you live on his chin?"

"I live in a real house," my brother's wife said. "That I own. That I paid for. With my job. Where do you live?"

"Here," I said, "with my dying or dead parents, alone, in a falling-down house that you are trying to sell."

"Shut up," said my brother.

"It's not yours to sell," I said, to my brother's wife.

"It's not yours to keep."

"It is not yours to sell."

"You're drunk," she said.

"You're a fucking bitch."

"Easy," my brother said. We were all silent for a moment.

"Yeah, I'm sorry," I said.

Then I took out a cigarette and lit it and inhaled and then exhaled the smoke right across the breakfast bar.

My brother's wife pushed her pizza plate away from herself. She stood up.

She looked at me and then she looked at my brother and then she walked out of the room and then we heard her go upstairs twice.

"You fucking gimp," my brother said.

Then he followed her out of the room.

I stayed in the kitchen and drank. I could hear them moving around upstairs in my parents' bedroom, arguing, walking on the old and softening wooden floorboards.

I felt sad and bad.

There were two fruit flies in the room, circling, occasionally landing on the cooling pizza to vomit fly sick onto it.

I gathered the pizza and put it into a bin bag. Then I took the bin bag and put it right into the outside bin.

That made me feel less like I was a bad person.

Then I lit another cigarette.

My brother and his wife stopped moving around and talking after a little while.

When they had I went upstairs.

I meant to go into my bedroom, but instead I went into my mother's study. I wanted to make sure the shoebox with the video was undisturbed.

The outside plants had managed to get into the study too, now. The wallpaper was peeling under the weight of the growing mold. The creeping figure in the pattern of it.

I turned on the lamp and opened my phone to look at the

photos I'd sent my brother of the video: my mother, and the foreign man, and the car, and the children who looked like the boy and the girl. But I couldn't find them. So I gave up. Instead, I opened the manuscript to the place I'd left off at.

CHAPTER THIRTEEN

Guy was so close.

The boy's skin was stretched wide, clamped end to end between sanitized metal. All his sweat was inside his gloves. Back behind an ear he felt the strap of a surgical mask open a sore. A moment. Then the drip of it on his neck.

He took the scissors to the boy's skin.

So close in the dream the night before. The induced paralysis. Forcing himself to submit to the no-movement.

The wetsuited man, steam or smoke coming off him, at the foot of his bed. Long-limbed and terrifyingly tall, shining black in the no-light. Tree roots growing fractal out of him, almost antlered. The smell of petrol, burned meats, plastic.

Unzipping his mouth to speak.

Guy's phone rang.

He peeled the gloves off his hands.

Rebecca had slept in her jeans and now her legs were sweating and stiff. Eighty-nine hours now Felix had been missing. She heard three rings and then Guy's voice.

"Rebecca," he said. He sounded out of breath, somehow. Muffled. She paused before speaking.

"Guy," she said.

"I didn't think you'd call. I'm so sorry about—"

Guy slipped the mask below his chin, feeling the sore behind his ear scraped by the strap.

"It doesn't matter," Rebecca said.

"I really just thought—I felt like I was somewhere else. I didn't mean anything by it."

Rebecca remembered the weight of Guy's body pushing her against the office wall. His pawing at her arms and shoulders and breasts. His wide-eyed, dejected, childlike face when she pushed away slightly. Tears welling in those eyes.

"Why are you calling? What can I help with?"

"It's Felix," she said. Rebecca felt tears in her eyes now.

Guy sat down in his chair. He felt his heart burning, trapped air escaping his throat.

"What about him?" he said.

"He's—" She swallowed. She realized she didn't know what she was doing. "Your patient—where is he? The patient that went missing. Has he been found?"

"God," Guy said.

"What?"

"They found him," Guy said, "but he's dead."

"Oh, God," Rebecca said. She felt herself begin to cry silently.

"He was in the sea. Washed ashore. He was wearing a wetsuit. With Russian writing on it. It said 'Leningrad' on it, or something. It seemed like he was trying to swim somewhere."

"Jesus," Rebecca said.

"Why are you asking? Is Felix—"

"Felix is missing," Rebecca said. She felt solid suddenly. As if she were a long-dead and petrified tree.

"Fucking hell," Guy said. He exhaled.

"I don't know what I'm doing."

"I'm so close," Guy said.

"More than three days," Rebecca said.

"I should have worked faster. I should have realized sooner."

"I'm in pieces," Rebecca said.

Guy thought about what he could say. He looked around the room for the right thing. It all sounded too insane.

"Felix's dreams," he said, "what did he say about them?"

"What? Um. A tree. Something about a car, maybe crashing. A deer. The house falling down."

"Christ," Guy said.

"What?" Rebecca said.

"I think—it's good news. I just need one more night."

"What? You know something? Have you done something?"

"What?" Guy said.

"Where's Felix?" Rebecca said, suddenly remembering the way Guy had put his face so close to Felix's skin, inhaled so deeply and intently and focused.

"I don't know. I promise. But give me one more night."

"The police are involved. If you know something you need to tell me."

"I wish I did. I promise. I wish I did. It's good the police are involved. One more night. I'll call in the morning."

After they hung up, Rebecca sat at the foot of Felix's bed, the black-out curtains closed to the daylight. She picked up his toy cat and sobbed.

That night, Guy swallowed the part of the boy whole.

It slipped down his throat like unchewed ham, settled in his emptied stomach.

He turned off the light and waited for sleep to take him, the burned and wetsuited man to appear standing at the foot of his bed, unzipping his own mouth to speak.

I woke up in my bedroom. My phone said it was 10:36 a.m., which seemed good. I lay there for a while. My head felt clear. Probably from drinking less than usual the night before.

I could hear something in the garden. The sound of rusted metal against metal, coming from the autumn trees and shrubbery right at the back. My bedroom window was open. So I looked out of it.

The shed door was closed still, like I'd left it, padlocked. I couldn't see the deer-man. Or anything.

But I closed the window still.

I thought about the manuscript for a while. The missing boy, his skin falling off. The mother and the strange scientist who seemed to be eating it. It wasn't my mother's best work.

I put on a T-shirt that said IN CASE OF DISHONOR CUT HERE in English and Japanese, with a dotted line across the stomach.

I went downstairs.

My brother's wife was in the kitchen.

"Coffee?" I said. She didn't say anything. My brother walked in as she walked out. He kissed her on the forehead as they passed.

"Make me coffee," my brother said.

I made us both coffee. I made a spitting sound and mimed spitting in one of the mugs. Then I handed it to my brother.

"I can't drink this," he said, "there's a gay man's spit in it."

My brother and his wife had brought loads of cardboard boxes. My brother told me to assemble them, which was fine. Assembling the boxes was good. They started off two-dimensional and became three-dimensional. I enjoyed slotting the tabs into the holes to connect the panels together. It reminded me of a job I'd had at a disgusting pizza place as a student.

I would build three in a row and then carry them up to the landing and fill them with books from the bookshelf there. I did not want to start on either of my parents' studies, or their bedroom, or my bedroom. It felt better to be packing books that were ambient books. Rather than books that belonged to someone in particular.

The wood of the bookshelves was softening, gnawed.

Behind the books the walls were wet and black.

After, I looked at the internet on my laptop. My girlfriend had a new story out, in a magazine I'd not heard of. I checked to see if I was still blocked and I was. But it was all over everyone else's Twitters.

I looked inside myself to see what I felt but then I stopped. I could feel my heart pushing my chest. I thought about closing the tabs and the laptop and never reading it. But instead I clicked one of them open and started reading.

ABOUT LOVE

The first time I fell in love I was eight. It was the summer. We summered with friends of my father's: a couple and their son, aged ten or eleven.

The son and I rode bicycles to a ramshackle amusement park, all wood and wasps and spilled ice cream.

I was very small and it seemed very, very big. We—me and the son—liked the teacups that spun, and the seats suspended from ropes that spiraled in the air, and the carousel animals. But most of all we liked the roller coaster.

It was so noisy. Wood on metal. A train going endlessly in one direction. We rode it first every day. Then we rode the other rides. Then we would ride our roller coaster again.

I remember sharing the coldest soda in the world. What a shoulder against a shoulder felt like.

I remember learning all the things that eyes can do.

One day, on the last ride of our roller coaster, just after the top, where I loved the empty feeling of my stomach being left somewhere behind me, I heard him whisper to me, barely audible, so quiet I wasn't even sure he said it: you are the most beautiful girl I have ever seen, and I am in love with you.

I think I left my stomach up there forever.

After we climbed out of the carriage I expected so much.

But the son acted no different.

As if he hadn't said anything at all.

The next day I was so sad. But I didn't show it. Again we rode our roller coaster.

And at the top, or just after it, barely audible, I thought I maybe heard him say it again: you are the most beautiful girl I have ever seen, and I am in love with you.

And I looked over at him and again he was looking right ahead, grinning.

And after we climbed out of the carriage he acted normally. As if he'd not said anything at all.

That was when I learned that you could be kept up at nights. Just by something someone had maybe said.

The rest of the holiday I was so sad. All the time. Except for when, each day, we were at the top of our roller coaster together, and I maybe heard the son say those words or maybe didn't.

And then when I would look over at him and see him grinning and looking right ahead all the sad would come rushing back.

And at the end of the journey home, after the holiday, at the ferry terminal, trying to catch his, I learned all the things that eyes can't do.

The second time I fell in love was with my family's groundskeeper. I was thirteen. He was forty. Or that's the age he was in my head.

We summered in our own country by then, in the house all my father's money had bought, on the land that all my father's money had bought.

The groundskeeper and my father were on good terms. Together they took their guns out.

The huge and muscled deer on the back of the jeep when they returned.

"If there were still wolves here," my father had said, "we wouldn't need to do this."

The taste of the bloodless meat of it in my throat.

The groundskeeper's dark forearms resting on our kitchen table.

I thought he was the ugliest man in the world.

The third time I fell in love was when I was Julie Christie in the movie *Don't Look Now*.

I was in love with Donald Sutherland. Donald Sutherland was my husband, and his job was to put broken churches back together.

We had a daughter together. A son, too.

But our daughter drowned in the lake on our land that all our money had bought.

And my husband's heart broke all at once, and forever, into a trillion tiny pieces.

That's the main difference between girls and boys: girls' heartbreaks take the longest time.

But boy hearts break all at once.

So we went to Italy, me and my husband, to a church that was broken and needed putting back together.

We tried to put his heart back together, too.

I tried so hard. But he was in a trillion tiny pieces.

And when I realized that he would spend forever putting his heart back together—

that it would take more time than the universe had—

I screamed and screamed for him, and for his heart, and for mine too, and for our daughter, stuck red-raincoated, forever left in our lake.

I was too late. He was already in too many pieces.

But how beautiful his half-built church was!

Here's something: I stole all these stories. They're not mine.

But also they are.

Here's something else: all the girls in the world leave their stomachs forever at the top of their first wooden roller coaster.

And I think often of the son grinning and looking straight ahead and that's what love is. The most cruel, the funniest joke in the world.

Another cruel and funny joke: all the boys in the world rest their dark-colored forearms on kitchen tables and never realize how ugly, how beautiful they are.

And I can write all the sentences in the world.

And I can scream and I can scream and I can scream.

And I can love all the trillion pieces of boys scattered, all their eyes and forearms.

Funny: that I can touch each of them. But not hold them.

That all it can ever be is a candle lit, a roller-coaster prayer, maybe misheard in a forever incomplete church.

I closed the tab and then closed my laptop.

I didn't think about anything. I just wanted to be somewhere else.

I went downstairs.

My brother was in the living room. I didn't know where his wife was.

"Where's your wife?" I said.

"Mum and Dad's room. What do you want?"

"I am going to go to the shop. To buy food. Maybe you want something."

"Cornetto."

"Anything else?"

"Big bags. Parcel tape. Ask my wife."

"She's angry at me," I said.

"She's angry at me," he said. "Apologize."

I walked out of the room and up the first set of stairs. The door to my mother's study was closed like I'd left it. I made a mouth noise and walked loudly up the second stairs to my parents' bedroom.

I pushed the door open.

My brother's wife was in there. The attic door was open. The grow tent was dismantled. The lights were all over the floor.

She had a pair of scissors in her hand.

The cannabis plants were cut at the base of their stems.

I could see them poking out of the top of a black-plastic bin bag. My brother's wife was cutting down the last one.

"What the fuck?" I said.

"What?" she said.

"You can't do that."

"Yes. I can."

"They're not yours to cut down," I said.

"Are you fucking with me?" she said.

I went over to where the bin bag was. She recoiled slightly. I pulled the bin bag open. I could see the dead plants and some soil. I put my hand on one of the plants.

"Dad grew these," I said.

"It's fucking illegal."

"You could have waited. Until they were finished."

She didn't say anything. She turned away from me and toward the last plant.

She cut it at the base of its stem. It was thick. She twisted the scissors around it.

It came apart and I heard the sound of it.

I sat down on the bed. On the back of the bedroom door I saw my father's bathrobe, still hanging there.

My face felt hot. I began to cry.

"You fucking bitch," I said. "You fucking bitch."

Have you been crying?" my grandmother said. "Every time you come here you've been in a fight. Or you're crying."

"I have not been crying," I said.

"Hm," my grandmother said. She hugged me a second time. I took off my shoes. "Go and sit down," she said.

I sat in the living room. It was raining again. She brought me some extremely strong instant coffee, a plate of biscuits.

"Thanks," I said. She smiled. She sat down in her chair. Her cat was sitting next to me, on the sofa. I put my hand lightly on its back.

"I remember when I first met your father," my grandmother said. "I was visiting your mother. At university. And she wanted to introduce him to me."

I said, "Hm."

"He was very polite, and very handsome. And very shy."

"He never seemed shy to me," I said.

"People aren't shy to their children," my grandmother said. "I remember he cycled to the restaurant where we met. When he stood up to leave, he still had his trouser leg tucked into his sock. To stop it getting caught in his bicycle chain. He must have forgotten about it. Maybe because he was so nervous. That made me like him very, very much."

I didn't say anything. I just sipped my coffee.

"I remember him most then, and I remember taking your brother to visit you and your mother in the hospital. Right after you were born. I was looking after your brother."

"I don't remember that," I said. She smiled.

"I remember showing you to your brother for the first time. I remember him holding you. He was so tired and handsome and happy."

"You remember good bits," I said. "I don't know what I remember. Everyone keeps saying things."

"When someone dies it becomes a competition to be in charge of the history of that person. People want their memory to be the real one."

"Hm," I said.

"It is ugly, but it's natural," she said. "But history is the opposite of memory. Each time you remember you rewrite. History only gets written a handful of times. The important thing is that you don't let other people affect your own memories. Those are the important things."

"Hm," I said, again.

We were silent for a moment.

"You know," she said, "memory is irrevocably wrapped in loss." She looked at me in my eyes. Then she looked away. "I worry about the future, sometimes. Everything is photographed. I can watch television shows from fifty years ago on the computer."

"Hm," I said.

"It's as if by losing nothing we are losing loss. And forgetting how to remember."

"What about the books you write?" I said. "If they mess up memory."

"Those are not memories," my grandmother said. "You know this really. They're imagination. That's something else. Another universe."

"It sounds bad for dead people," I said. "History."

"Maybe," she said. She smiled.

"I hope I die before you," I said, looking down.

Then I turned to the cat and put my face in its coat and said it again.

The rain outside, the purring sound of it.

It was dark when I got back to the house. The light in the living room was on. But the other lights seemed to be off.

The plants were all up the side of the front of the house now, as if suffocating the peeling brickwork.

The holes in the roof where the tiles had fallen seemed bigger.

I opened the front door quiet.

I took off my shoes and went into the living room where the light was.

My brother was alone in there. He sat on the sofa in Dad's spot. The television was on. It was showing *Deadliest Warrior*. He was drinking whisky that I didn't know had been in the house. There was an empty bottle of red wine beside him, too.

I sat next to him on the sofa.

I put the plastic bag from the shop on the floor in front of me.

I got one of the Cornettos I'd bought out of the bag and handed it to my brother. He looked at it then took it. Then he looked at me for a second. Then he unwrapped the Cornetto and began eating it.

I took another Cornetto out of the bag and unwrapped it and began eating it, too.

"There's one for your wife," I said.

On the television, a man swung a samurai sword into a hanging pig carcass. The pig was cut immediately in two. The bottom half of the pig fell on the floor.

"See that?" my brother said, gesturing with the Cornetto.

"Yeah," I said.

"You can't fuck with the samurai."

"Hm," I said.

"They were the perfectly optimized soldier," my brother said, "to deal with the existential threat dead pigs posed to medieval Japan."

"Where's your wife?" I said.

"This show is so good," my brother said. "I need to watch more TV."

"Yeah," I said.

"I drove her to the station," he said. "She's going back to London. I thought it was best we do this. Just us."

"Her Cornetto will melt," I said.

"Don't worry," my brother said, "I will eat it for her."

"It was Dad's idea," I said.

"What?" my brother said.

"Do you remember Aunty Sally's funeral? Everyone was fighting. About money. I think. And Dad disappeared for fifteen minutes and then came back with a plastic bag full of Creme Eggs. And he handed everyone a Creme Egg. And then nobody could keep fighting because they would look too stupid. Because they were eating Creme Eggs. It would have been too funny. To fight while eating a Creme Egg."

"I'd forgotten that," my brother said.

"I think about it whenever I eat Creme Eggs. Or whenever I'm fighting."

"No wonder you lose so often," my brother said. He took a bite of the Cornetto and then a drink of the whisky. On television they were swinging a Viking ax against a new dead pig.

"Are you really going to eat two Cornettos?" I said. "Your brain will freeze."

"Yeah," said my brother.

"Can I have some whisky?" I said.

He said yeah again and passed me the bottle. I drank a little bit from it.

"I'm sorry, obviously," I said.

"For calling my wife a bitch?"

"Yeah," I said.

"For repeatedly calling my wife a bitch?"

"Yeah," I said.

"You're sorry for what? What?" he said, miming that he couldn't hear.

"For repeatedly calling your bitch wife a bitch," I said.

"Thank you," he said.

On the television, a man swung a samurai club against a gel torso. The samurai club was wooden, with little metal rivets.

It smashed the gel torso's head to smithereens.

My brother started laughing.

"That was so Dad," my brother said, "the Creme Eggs."

I laughed, too.

"Yeah," I said, "I wonder if Mum remembers."

"Probably, sometimes," my brother said. He was silent for a moment.

"I'm so scared of the day she forgets who we are," he said.

"She won't forget you," I said.

"I'm not so sure," my brother said.

"She won't," I said, "you're too ugly."

When I woke up, someone was knocking on the door. I thought: my brother will answer the door. I looked at the clock. It said 1:26 p.m. My head hurt.

The knocking kept happening, with shorter and shorter intervals between bouts of knocks.

I put on my yesterday clothes and went downstairs.

When I opened the door, the boy was there. Behind him I saw the metallic-blue car parked. The girl in the passenger seat.

I said hey and he said it back, quiet.

"You have red wine on your teeth," he said. I wiped my mouth. Then I bared my teeth at him.

"How about now?"

"Yeah, no change."

"What do you want?"

"Want to take a drive?"

"I have to put all my dead parents' stuff into boxes," I said.

"Don't do that. Do this."

I looked behind me, into the house. I felt a cold wind coming from the inside, somehow.

I imagined my brother sleeping, all the way at the top of the house, in our parents' bed. He had been so drunk.

"Sure," I said. "Whatever."

We drove into the city. It took a little while. There was some traffic. The air was cold but the top of the car was down. The stereo was off. The girl had moved to the back. I sat up front.

I wished I'd brought sunglasses.

I didn't say anything. The boy didn't say anything either. Then the girl told me that I looked a little better.

"You look a little better," she said.

"Thanks," I said.

"But you usually have vomit on your shirt, or blood, or something."

"You can't see his teeth," the boy said.

"I haven't thrown up in a while. Or been punched."

"You get into a lot of fights," the boy said.

I said, "Not really fights."

We reached the part of the city where the university campus was.

"My mother used to teach here," I said, "before she was demented."

"Teach what?" the girl said.

"English. Creative Writing."

"Can you write?" the girl said.

"Not really," I said, "I'm just good at pretending."

"We grew up really close to here," the boy said, "our parents taught here."

We pulled up beside a bus stop. To the left was the university library, a big building made of red bricks. There were delicate shrubs and a bust of someone and abstract sculptures all around. A sundial.

On the right there was a huge swimming pool building made of glass.

I wanted to swim.

"You recognize this?" the boy said.

"Yeah," I said.

There were students waiting at the bus stop. Chinese ones and English ones, too. They were looking at big phones or talking to each other or staring off into the middle distance with earphones in.

We were silent for a while. We sat with the engine idling. The boy looked up at the sky. I looked up at it, too.

It was an almost transparent blue, cloudless, crisscrossed with dissipating airplane trails.

A bus arrived behind us.

We pulled away.

The boy drove out of the city, into the forest. The air was cold around my head, the way it is in autumn.

I put my hand above the windshield to catch it.

It slipped through, like it does.

We turned off a big road onto a small road.

The small road was only wide enough for one car. There were hedgerows on either side of us. We went down it for a little while slowly. There were no other cars.

We reached a small lay-by. The boy pulled over. He turned

off the engine. In front of us and to the right was a dead tree. It was all gnarled, black and gray, becoming petrified. It was very quiet. I could hear birds and the wind in hedgerows.

"You recognize it here?" the girl said.

"No," I said. "I've never been here."

"We have. When we were very young. A lot of times. But first when we were very young."

"Okay," I said.

"When we were very young," the girl said, "we had horrible dreams. We dreamed that our mother had gotten into a car with a man who was not our father. And a deer ran out in front of the car, and then the car hit that tree."

"I've heard this story before," I said.

"We dreamed that our mother was dying on the road here, under that tree. That nobody would save her. Except us. And one day, when the dreams got too much, we left in the middle of the night. To save her."

"Did you?" I said.

"We had to hide whenever we saw grown-ups. It took us two days to walk out here. We knew people would be looking for us. Our dad, the police. We were very tired and very, very hungry."

"But did you?"

"It was daytime when we got here. Sunny, like now. We came around that corner expecting to see a car, smashed up. And our mother lying in the road, dying or dead. But there was nothing. Just that tree there, alive. And a deer walking across the road."

"So we sat near the tree, waiting for the car to show up."

"But it never came."

"Why is the tree dead now?" I said.

"A couple of years later," the boy said, "our mother got into a car with a man who wasn't our father. And he drove her out here. And something happened, and the car hit that tree. And they both died."

"Seriously?" I said.

"We got the right place. But not the right time."

"I thought I'd heard this story before," I said, "but now I don't think it's the same."

"Our dad couldn't keep it together. He was too broken. He sold the house. He's gone, too. And now we're stuck."

"You need the house," one of them said. "That's what we're telling you. Or you will end up stuck."

"Stuck?" I said.

But neither of them replied. The boy just started silently reversing back down the narrow road.

My brother was at the breakfast bar drinking coffee and looking at his phone.

"You go out?" he said.

I walked up to him and made an "okay" sign with my hand and held it slightly below him so he couldn't see it.

"To the shop. I got you this."

He turned to look at my hand so I punched him in the arm.

"Ow," he said. "Dickhead."

"Those are the rules."

"I feel like shit."

"Good. Let's not do any work today."

"We've got Germany," he said, meaning football. "I'm having a beer after this coffee."

"That will help."

"Did Dad ever tell you that story about shooting a German exchange student with an air rifle?"

"Yeah," I said. It was one of our favorites. "He went blind. In one eye."

"Yeah," my brother said. Then he crossed his arms on the breakfast bar and put his head down on his arms. He moaned.

"I hope we don't lose today," he said.

My brother went back to bed. He told me to put more stuff in boxes. But I looked at my laptop instead.

I was scared of what the boy and girl had said. That I needed to keep the house and that I needed to look after it.

In my email there was a message from my agent. He wanted to know where my book was at, how much progress had been made.

I had still not done any work at all.

I thought about ignoring the email.

Instead I wrote back that I was sorry, that I had something really special, and that I'd send it to him next week, once I'd worked out some structural problems.

Once I hit send I felt good. Like I'd done something.

I went downstairs. The air was full of dust floating.

I opened a beer and put the pre-match coverage on and waited for my brother to wake up, and come downstairs, and watch football with me, how we used to.

If we lose I am going to kill myself," I said.

This was an old joke we liked to make.

"Do it anyway," my brother said. "Do it when Mum dies. We can throw you a joint funeral."

"That could be years," I said, "and I would have to watch more football in the meantime."

"Kill me first, before you, then."

I said, "How?"

"Actually, do not kill me. You would fuck it up."

"I can use a samurai sword. To seppuk-you. Or I could use one of the clubs they had with the metal spikes."

A gambling advert was on television. In white writing on a blue background it said: *when the fun stops, stop.*

"Jesus," said my brother. He tucked his chin into the jumper he was wearing. It looked like one of Dad's jumpers.

"When the fun stops, stop," I said. Then I mimed smashing a gel torso's head with a Japanese spike club. "That was your head," I said, "your head was smashed in."

"Jesus," said my brother.

"They should do a *Deadliest Warrior* that is just me and you. Simulate the fight one thousand times. On a supercomputer."

"I would win," said my brother.

"No, you wouldn't win. I would win all one thousand simulated fights. A crushing defeat."

"You can't even win against an estate agent. Or my teenage son."

"He's quite strong," I said. My brother curled his arm.

"Like his father," he said.

"I would not even need any weapons," I said. "You see these hands?" I stretched out my arms and wrists.

"These hands?" my brother said, in the Robert De Niro voice.

"These hands are registered as deadly weapons. Extremely deadly. I have to register them for some reason. With the government."

"These hands?" my brother said, in the Robert De Niro voice. "Yeah, they're registered with the government. Registered as extremely gay. Because they masturbate so many men."

"Yes, your hands are gay," I said.

"I've simulated one thousand sexual encounters with men," my brother said, still using the voice, "and in each encounter these hands masturbated the man, or men, to orgasm."

The football match started.

"Your hands are gay," I said. "Mine are deadly."

"You are the reason there's no show called *Gayest Man*," my brother said. "Because everyone already knows who the gayest man in history is."

"You?" I said.

My brother finished his beer and stood to get another. Once he left the room the Germans scored. Eight minutes of the game had passed. He came back into the room with two beers.

"Fucking hell," he said.

"Why would you leave the room like that?"

"Shut up," he said. He handed me one of the beers and sat down and put his chin back into the jumper. I opened my new beer.

We sat in silence until half-time.

The Germans scored two more. The stadium booed when the players went back into the dressing room.

"Kraut cunts," my brother said.

"I hate football," I said, "and I am going to kill myself."

"Shut up," my brother said. He muted the television when the advertisements came on and closed his eyes. It was very quiet. I smelled mold smell in the inside wind. I lit a cigarette.

"Can you not do that?" my brother said.

"Do what?"

"Smoke. Indoors."

"Dad did."

"We're trying to sell the house. You're not Dad," my brother said.

"Neither are you," I said, "you are just wearing his jumper."

"Shut up."

"Sorry, you want one?" I said. I shook the pack at him. "You just had to ask."

"Shut up."

"This could be you," I said, and pointed to the health warning on the packet of cigarettes. It was a pair of naked legs with a cigarette burn where the genitals should be.

"I'm already done," my brother said. "I have procreated. I don't need it anymore."

"So smoke," I said.

"I'm vasectomized," my brother said. "It's handled."

"I didn't know that," I said.

"Yeah," my brother said.

"What is it like?"

"A lot like being you, I imagine," my brother said.

"You must feel excellent," I said.

The players came back out for the second half.

"Actually I do not feel excellent," my brother said. "I piss off people's wives. And cry like a bitch when people's wives chop down illegal cannabis plants. And have weird complexes about my skin. And make up weird stories about it."

"It's not a story," I said, "it's real. All my skin is peeling off."

Jadon Sancho scored for England. He picked the ball out of the net and ran with it back into the center circle and placed it on the spot for the Germans to kick off.

"Great," my brother said, "now we have to have hope again."

"It is all peeling off. I promise. And my leg got infected. But I peeled the infection right off. Like I'm Wolverine."

"Jordan Henderson is a fucking clown," my brother said.

"And it's happening to a character in one of Mum's manuscripts, too. I can show you the manuscript. But she does not remember writing it. She thinks it's a different book. It's about a boy whose skin is all peeling off. He goes missing. And the mum, in the book, has to find him. With the help of a gross scientist."

"This isn't funny," my brother said.

"I am not being funny," I said. "The manuscript keeps changing. Or it changed once. And in Dad's study there's a story about a VHS tape that keeps changing. This morning a boy and girl came to the house. While you were asleep. I think they're the boy and girl in the book. Their mum died in a car crash, too. Like in the book Mum thinks she wrote. But his skin didn't peel off, I don't think. Just mine."

"This is not funny," my brother said, "and I don't know if you're joking."

"I am not joking," I said. "I can show you the manuscript. I can show you the skin next time it happens. You can meet the boy and girl. When they come round again. And I can show you the video. You've seen the pictures of it."

"I think you should see a doctor," my brother said.

"They say we can't sell the house. I need to look after it. Or something really bad will happen. I'm serious."

"Right," my brother said, "that's what this is about."

"Yes. But not like that. I'm scared. I don't know what's going to happen to me. Without the house. You've seen what's happening to it. It's like my skin. It's like me."

"That's what this is about," my brother said.

"Yes. But not like that."

"My wife just lost her job," my brother said.

"What?" I said.

"She lost her job," he said. "Last month."

"I didn't know that," I said, because I didn't.

"Yeah, well. Now you know. We need to. Don't make me choose between supporting my family and your insane, grieving bullshit. Because I will look after my family."

"It's real. I'm scared."

"You need to talk to a doctor."

"You are a doctor. And I don't need to. It's real. I can show you."

My brother straightened his back. He turned his head to look at me in my eyes.

"You're grieving," he said, "that's all. People do it in different ways. But you need to see a doctor. For your head and your skin."

"I am grieving. But this is not a facet of that."

"People grieve in different ways. And you are grieving very weirdly."

"This is not a facet of that," I said.

"I cried like a bitch when I heard Dad died. I got drunk and drove to a lay-by in the country and cried like a bitch. For two hours. It's okay."

"You shouldn't drink-drive," I said.

"You shouldn't drive. Because you can't even drive."

"You never taught me," I said. "Nobody ever taught me."

"You have all your book money," he said. "It's not as easy for everyone else. Some people have to actually have jobs. You think I want to sell this place? I need to."

"I didn't know that. But we can't."

"We can, and we will. And everything will be fine. And in a couple of years we will laugh about this together."

"I'm scared," I said. "Please."

"You need to talk to a doctor."

"You are a doctor. And you are my brother. Why won't you believe me? I am frightened."

"I am not qualified to help you with this. You need to understand that."

On the television Germany scored again.

"Fuck's sake," my brother said. "Fucking fuck."

I finished my beer.

I stood up and left the room.

I badly rolled a joint and took it out into the back garden. The air was getting colder.

I shivered.

The cold made me feel very small.

I felt frightened and drunk and embarrassed.

I lit the joint. It tasted bad. The roach was too loose. My tongue burned. There was the sound of the motorway far off.

In less than thirty seconds I felt stoned.

I heard something move in the growing bushes and shrubbery and gray-black trees at the bottom of the garden.

I knew exactly what it was.

But I just thought: let it watch.

I thought about Christmases I would spend at home from university, years before. Smoking in the garden, looking out into the black, just like now.

Going out for a cigarette or joint and Dad joining me, drunk and sheepish in a cardigan and Crocs, two or three minutes later. Then my brother too, sometimes, if his wife and son were asleep.

And I would finish my cigarette, and then just stand there watching them smoke theirs, until they finished, and I would love them both so much that my heart hurt.

And then we would go back inside to where my mother was waiting for us all.

In the living room I picked up the remote and turned the television to the VHS input.

"What the fuck?" my brother said.

"I need to show you this," I said.

"I was watching that. It's England. You should be, too."

"It's five–one. And it's not going to get any better."

"I'm not indulging this," my brother said.

"Please," I said, "don't be a prick."

"I am not indulging this," my brother said. "I am going to watch the football."

"If I am wrong, then I am wrong, and then I will go to a doctor," I said. "But you need to look at this first."

"I've seen this. You sent photos to me."

"But not the manuscript. You don't know what they mean. Because you haven't seen the manuscript."

My brother put his head into his hands. He exhaled. Then he rubbed his eyes. Then he looked back up. But at the television. Not at me.

"Fine," my brother said, "whatever. Let's do it."

"Thank you," I said.

"But you are going to talk to a doctor. And tomorrow we are going to finish clearing out this house and we are going to sell it."

I thought about what the boy and girl had said and how scared I was. But I didn't know what else I could do.

"If you still want to after, that's okay."

"Okay," my brother said.

I put the tape that I'd retrieved from upstairs into the player.

I pressed play.

Snowstorm appeared.

I waited for the start of the video. My mother's lap, and then my father's face, and then my brother grinning, running toward the camera. But it didn't start.

I looked at my brother. But he didn't look at me. He took a drink.

I could hear the tape running in the player.

I waited.

"Is this the right tape?" my brother said.

"Wait," I said.

"Okay," he said.

I looked at the television. Then I looked back at him. Black and white flickered on his face.

I heard the tape stop in the player.

"Right," my brother said.

"No," I said, "hang on."

"You see how this looks," my brother said.

"No," I said. "This happens. In Dad's script. I told you about this. It's just happening here."

"It's a blank tape," my brother said.

"It's not," I said.

"You're sure you got the right one?" he said.

"Yes. This shows it's the right one."

"You see how this looks," my brother said.

"You're not listening," I said.

My brother made a mouth noise.

"Rewind it," he said. "Maybe I missed something."

He stood up and went to get another beer.

"That's not how this works," I said. I rewound it anyway. I pressed play. Snowstorm filled the screen again.

My brother walked back into the room with two beers and two glasses of whisky.

"Two drinks," he said, "remember?"

"Don't patronize me."

"I'm listening. I'm watching the tape. This is what we agreed. I'm trying to be nice."

"You're not listening," I said.

"I am," he said. He put all the drinks down on the coffee table.

"You're not," I said. The screen was still full of snowstorm.

"Are we done?" my brother said. "Have a drink."

"The manuscript. The manuscript, too. In Mum's study. You have to look at that, too. Please."

Then the snowstorm stopped, and our mother's lap appeared.

"See?" I said.

The camera turned to our father. He made his funny face into it. Then he smiled.

"I don't need to see this," my brother said.

"You do," I said.

I waited for the camera to turn to my brother. But it didn't. The tape just stopped there, right on our father, young and handsome, smiling at us out of the television.

The image stayed on the television, shuddering.

"I really don't need to see this," my brother said.

"It changed," I said. "You saw it before. It changed."

My brother sat down on the sofa. He looked at Dad. Then he looked over at me.

"You get this is horrible for me, right?" he said.

"What?" I said.

"I don't want to look at this," he said.

I looked over at Dad. He shuddered on the screen, stuck mid-smile.

Then the snowstorm reappeared.

I felt bad.

"Right," I said. "I'm sorry."

"I mean, Jesus fucking Christ," my brother said.

"It's okay. I'll turn it off. I'm sorry. But you need to look at the manuscript, too."

We went up the stairs and into my mother's study. I went first. I wanted to look back at my brother to check if he was still there. But I didn't. I just listened to his footsteps.

"Sit down," I said. "It's that one."

I'd turned the manuscript all the way back to the front, to the title page.

"Yeah," my brother said.

He sat down at the desk and turned on the desk lamp. I leaned against the wall by the door. I felt it move behind me, a shift, a sinking.

The shade on the lamp gave the room an almost transparent, blue glow. My brother looked down at the title page.

I felt frightened. I didn't know which version of the manuscript he'd see. It could be the version I'd read first, the one my mother had told me about on the phone. Or it could be the strange story I'd read about the skinless boy who goes missing. Or it could be something else altogether.

"*A Bit of Earth*," my brother said.

"That's right," I said. He turned to me.

"Do I have to read it aloud?"

"Shut up," I said.

"Not aloud," he said, "got it."

He looked back down at the title page again. Then he turned back to me.

"What?" I said. He made a slightly pained face. Then he composed himself.

"I'm doing this because I love you," he said. "But it is really fucking horrible for me."

"I know," I said.

"I don't think you do," he said.

"I'm sorry," I said. I felt bad.

"Like, really fucking horrible."

"I'm sorry," I said, again. "She's not dead yet."

"Yeah," my brother said. He looked at the title page then back at me again.

"Just read it," I said, "please. And if you still think I'm being whatever I will do whatever you want. I'll stop bothering you. I'll see a doctor."

"And the house," my brother said.

"Yeah," I said.

"Okay," my brother said. He turned back to the manuscript so I couldn't see his face.

I closed the door behind me.

The football was over on the television. The news was on. A volcano had erupted in New Zealand. Wild dogs had taken over a Scottish town. A million tubes of moisturizer were washing ashore, off the back of some capsized container ship.

I didn't want to watch that so I went out into the garden to smoke another cigarette. The garden was very dark still. I thought about my brother alone, upstairs, reading; the room blue from the light from the lamp.

The cigarette got short quick. I moved my fingers so I didn't burn them.

The back door opened behind me loud.

I turned.

"Is this some kind of fucking sick joke?" my brother said. He had the manuscript in his hand.

"What?" I said. "What version did you get?"

"There's nothing here. There's nothing in it. It's not a book. It's just the same page over and over."

"What?"

"You're fucked. In the head. Or you have been lying to me. Which is it?"

"Show me," I said. He handed the manuscript to me, then turned around.

I opened the manuscript.

"You probably printed this. You can't even put effort into a sick fucking joke."

He was right. It wasn't a manuscript at all. It was just the title page over and over, maybe three hundred or three hundred and fifty times, each set alone in black on its own bright white page.

My brother came back toward me.

"So, what the fuck?" he said.

"This is like the tape in Dad's script. At the end of it. And the tape just now. Just the beginning over and over."

"What?" my brother said. "It's not like anything. You printed this out."

"You haven't read Dad's script," I said.

"No," my brother said. "That's enough. Either you fucking printed this out, or our demented mother did. And now you're making up some sick shit to fuck with me. So I don't sell this place. You need to see a fucking head doctor."

"I don't. Don't you see? The tape literally changed just now. It was blank before. Then we saw Dad."

"I left the room and you switched the fucking tapes."

"It happens in Dad's script, too. It changes. There's something bigger going on."

My brother took a step toward me and pushed me in the chest.

"This is fucked up. Stop fucking with me. It's enough."

"It will be there. You just need to read it again, maybe. It changes."

"Shut up," my brother said. He pushed me again.

"It's in there. And I can show you my skin. And you can talk to the boy. We need to look after the house. We can't sell it."

"Shut the fuck up," my brother said, "I'm not being funny."

"You've seen the video. You saw it change. It doesn't make sense."

"I don't care about the video."

"You should. You do care. Or you wouldn't be so angry."

"I don't care. Except that you are fucking with me. And fucking with my family."

"I am your family."

"This is what family does?"

"I've seen it change. And Mum remembers writing it. Ask her."

"She's sick and so are you."

"I'm not sick. I'm fine. I'm right."

"This is not right. This is cruel. My wife was right. This is unhealthy. You're just trying to get attention."

"I'm not," I said. "That's not fair. You're not being fair."

"I've been too fair. Once this is over, it's over. The house. This isn't what family does."

"It's not over. How can you not see that? You're so fucking stupid."

"Shut up," my brother said. He pushed me in the chest again.

Then he snatched the manuscript out of my hand and threw it against the wet ground hard.

The bright white pages scattered on the black. They moved in the wind.

"You just don't want me to be right. Because this works for you. Mum is sick and Dad is dead and I'm crazy."

"I don't think you're crazy," he said, "I think you're cruel."

"Why the fuck would I do this?" I said.

"To get what you want. To get whatever stupid fucking thing you want."

"I don't want this," I said.

"You don't want to sell. You hate my wife. You hate my family."

"I am your family."

"Are you?" he said. "Are you fucking really? He's my dad. Do you really think he's yours?"

In the bathroom we cleaned the blood off our faces. One of my front teeth felt loose. But I tried moving it and it stayed in me.

I looked at my brother in the mirror. We made eye contact through the mirror and then I looked away. Then I looked back at him and used my front tooth to flick my thumbnail in the direction of the mirror, in the direction of his reflection. My right hand hurt where I had hit him in the side of the head without closing my fist properly.

My brother did the same back at me, then made a face like he was in pain.

I made the same face back, exaggerated, to make fun of him.

He stepped away from the mirror, toward the door.

"Clean the sink," he said, and then left the room.

I ran the cold tap hard.

The spiraling water turned from clear to pink, and then back to clear again.

My hand kept hurting even after my brother left the room. I looked at it.

I noticed that there was a rift of skin, lifting above the little bone bump on my wrist.

I turned the hot tap on and put my hand under it. The water burned a bit. But I left my hand under it.

I felt it moving underneath my skin.

The skin started to come away by itself. I took my hand out from underneath the tap. I wanted the old skin gone. But I did not want it to disintegrate in the water.

I dug the thumbnail of my other hand underneath the rift.

Slowly it peeled away, like Sellotape.

The skin stopped peeling at the base of my knuckles. It started to sting.

The sink was cold. I used it as a pivot to break the skin off my hand. I pulled all of it off that would come, until I had a sheet of my own skin in my left hand that matched perfectly with the skin from the top of my right.

I held the sheet of skin up to the light.

It was so thin.

I thought about my brother. He would still be awake, lying on our parents' bed, drunk, maybe looking at his phone, or just into the black.

I wanted to show him the skin. To prove that I was right.

But instead I dropped the skin into the sink. It hit the porcelain. The sound was almost silent. I turned on the hot tap again and watched my skin disintegrate, into a trillion tiny pieces, and get carried into the deep black drain.

I stood for a moment watching the water spiral. Then I turned the tap off and went downstairs and into the garden to save the hundreds of identical and scattered and damp manuscript pages that we had left out there in the potentially raining night.

I woke to a knock on the door. I thought it was the front door at first. But then I realized it was my bedroom door.

I didn't remember falling asleep. Beside me was half of one of the big pink Xanax bars. I felt groggy.

I checked my pillow for blood. There was a little blood. But I didn't know if it was from last night. Or if it was older blood.

"What?" I said, to the door.

My brother said, "Supermarket."

"What time is it?" I said.

"Supermarket time," my brother said. "Get up."

"Supermarket time?" I said.

"Look alive," my brother said, through the door.

"I'll pretend," I said. But he didn't say anything back.

Then a moment passed and I heard him walking down the stairs.

I put on jeans and the T-shirt with all the Phils on it. I hadn't washed it since the day of the wake. But it didn't smell bad. It had come around the other side. Or the whole room smelled bad.

My brother was in the kitchen. He was holding a cup of coffee. And there was a second, full cup of coffee on the breakfast bar.

"Coffee," he said. "Drink it."

"Don't tell me what to do," I said.

"Do you ever shower?" he said. He had a cut under his eye too, and some bruising around it.

"Why would I?" I said.

"Drink the coffee," my brother said. I sat down at one of the breakfast barstools and picked up the coffee cup. Then I sipped it.

"It's too hot," I said, then grinned at him. Grinning made the cut on my face hurt.

"Shut up," my brother said.

My brother drove to the big supermarket. We had shopped there as children. It was a building on its own, surrounded by pine trees, strange scrubland. There wasn't really anything else around it until you got to the motorway.

"Were you there the time Dad ran out of fuel?" I said. "He ran out of fuel on this roundabout."

"No," my brother said. "He ran out of fuel?"

"The car stopped. The big white Volvo."

"The Great White Polar Bear," my brother said, remembering the car's name.

"Right in the middle of the roundabout," I said.

"I wasn't there."

"Dad was really angry. He hit the steering wheel. Then he looked at me and started laughing so I started laughing, too. People were honking."

"The Asda has a petrol station."

"Yeah," I said. "He got me out of the back of the car and we walked down the road together to the Asda petrol station. To buy petrol for the Polar Bear. I asked if the car would be okay there. He said that the car didn't matter because it didn't have any fuel in it."

"That's good," my brother said. "The car doesn't matter because it doesn't have any fuel in it."

We sat in silence for a moment at a red light.

"I once dreamed he'd taken down all the clocks in the house," my brother said, "to evade social obligations."

"What?" I said.

"If someone asked him to do something social, in the dream, he wanted to say: *sorry, I can't do that, I don't have any clocks.*"

"No fuel, no clocks," I said. "Good."

"He was a fucking idiot," my brother said, "that car was always overheating. Because he refused to put water in it. To cool it."

"I know why people put water in cars," I said.

"Dad didn't think it needed it," my brother said.

"I think he forgot," I said, "not refused."

"Maybe," my brother said.

We sat in silence for a moment.

"If the car overheated," I said, "he wouldn't have to go anywhere."

"That's very true," my brother said. "A cunning plan."

The supermarket was busy. I realized it was a Sunday. We parked far away from the entrance, almost next to the pine-tree scrubland. I wondered why the leaves on the pine trees weren't dead yet. Then I remembered that they didn't die in autumn. They stayed there all winter.

My brother locked the car and we walked toward the entrance. He was limping slightly. I didn't remember him falling the night before.

We took a trolley from the concatenated trolley chain and walked through the supermarket airlock area into the supermarket.

It was colder in there.

"I want a cauliflower," my brother said. He picked up a cauliflower wrapped in cellophane and put it into the trolley.

"Don't get any lettuce," I said. "I heard it's infectious."

My brother picked up some expensive plastic-covered tomatoes. Then he hunched his shoulders, like Dad did.

"Pomodorini," he said, loudly, in a bad version of Dad doing a bad Italian accent. Then he threw the tomatoes into the trolley. They bounced off the cauliflower, potentially bruising against woven metal.

I hunched my shoulders together and did the Italian hand thing.

"Hey, fuck your mother," I said, in the voice.

"Your dad's a finook," my brother said.

"He is not alive no more, hey?" I said.

A woman in a purple fleece sniffed at us to watch our language, then wheeled her trolley quickly away from us, toward the simulated hot-bakery area.

Fucking old bitch," my brother said. He pulled out the chair from underneath the circular supermarket canteen table. "I should have sparked her out."

"Yeah," I said. I sat down at the canteen table.

"Let's slash her tires," my brother said, toward the car park.

I looked at the now-bagged shopping in the trolley beside the canteen table. I worried about the frozen things. We seemed to have bought too much food.

"We bought too much food," I said.

"We bought the correct amount of food," my brother said. "We should've bought more food."

"Are we having a party?" I said.

"Yeah. You're not invited. Stay in your room."

"Free house," I said. "We should have a party."

"You can invite all of your friends," my brother said, sarcastically.

"I have friends," I said. We were quiet for a moment.

"I love supermarkets," my brother said. "Why can't I live here?"

"They do have everything," I said.

"They have everything. They have everything in them. I love that."

"Yeah," I said.

"Why don't you have a family yet? Get a family. Nothing feels better than being alone at a supermarket buying food for your family. I'm not joking."

"I thought I was going to," I said, "with my girlfriend."

"Right, sorry," my brother said. "What a fucking bitch."

I shrugged.

I looked down at all the shoppers. From the canteen's mezzanine level you could see almost all of the aisles, with all the people and their trolleys moving up and down them, like brightly colored mice in an extremely solvable and rewarding science maze.

My brother pulled my plate of canteen chips toward him.

"This was my favorite part of supermarket time," my brother said. "When Dad bought us chips and then did this. To cool them down."

My brother began breaking my chips in half, one by one. Steam came out of them.

"Yeah," I said.

I pulled his plate of chips toward me and started breaking them in half, too. The tips of my fingers burned a little. I watched the steam disappear into the carefully conditioned supermarket air.

My brother turned down a quiet country road and pulled into a lay-by. He motioned for me to look at him. He pointed at his legs.

"Accelerator," he said, moving one leg. "Brake."

"What?" I said. He pointed at the gear thing.

"It's in park. You put your foot on the brake and then put it in D. Then you lift your foot slowly. You don't need to accelerate. It does that itself."

"Right," I said.

He ran his hands around the steering wheel in each direction.

"That way goes left, that way goes right."

"Okay," I said.

My brother opened his door and got out. I did the same. We walked around the car. He didn't smile as we passed.

I sat down and closed the door.

"Seat belt," he said.

"I'm going to crash your car," I said.

"No, you're not," my brother said.

I put my foot on the brake pedal.

"D is for drive?" I said.

"Yep."

"What's R for? Retard?"

"Oui. It could be. It's a go-kart. Accelerate, brake. You can do it."

I pushed the gear thing into D. Then I lifted my brake foot slowly. I could feel my leg shaking.

The car moved forward like it was magic.

"You've got it," my brother said. "Try accelerating."

I lightly pushed down with my forward foot.

"Yeah," my brother said.

I turned the wheel slightly to see what it did to the car.

"You've got it, you've got it," my brother said.

Hedgerows started passing us faster. Under me I could feel the car against the road. I pushed down harder and watched the digital speedometer count three, five, eight, thirteen.

And when I turned to grin at my brother he was grinning too, and looking right ahead.

My grandmother came to the door with a scarf.

"My grandsons," she said. "A lovely surprise."

"We bought too much food, Grandma," my brother said, too loud. "So we brought you the good stuff."

"I have shopping," our grandmother said. She hugged my brother. Then she hugged me. "Have you been fighting?"

"No," I said.

"You should see the other guy," my brother said, gesturing at me.

Our grandmother looked at me. Then she looked at my brother.

"Every time," she said, to me. Then she looked at my brother. "You should know better," she said, to him.

"He started it," my brother said, "and I finished it."

"It looks like a draw to me," she said, "but you two never used to fight so much."

"We're the same size now," I said. "It wouldn't have been fair before."

"I'm bigger," my brother said.

"You're fatter," I said. Our grandmother made an annoyed sound.

"Bring the shopping inside," she said. "Then sit down. And stop it."

We unpacked the shopping into the cupboards and fridge and then went into the living room and sat on the sofa. I realized it was not raining like usual. But there were clouds going across the sky fast. Our grandmother asked us whether we wanted tea or coffee and we both said coffee and then she left and we heard the kettle start.

The cat walked into the room. It looked at both of us, then away. I hoped it would come over. But instead it jumped up onto the windowsill and sat, watching the garden birds.

Our grandmother brought a tray with three cups of coffee and biscuits on it into the room.

"Here," she said, smiling. She handed us the coffee. Then she sat down.

I puffed out my cheeks at my brother to make a fat-guy face to make fun of him. But he ignored me.

"How's the writing, Grandma?" he said, too loud.

I expected her to put her hands on the side of her head and make an arrrrgkh sound. But she didn't. She just did a half smile.

"It's finished," she said. "I sent it off Friday."

"Really?" I said.

"Yes," she said, smiling.

"How do you feel?"

"Tired," she said. "Exhausted. But in a good way. Like I spent the afternoon in the sun."

"I read some of it," I said, "sorry."

"That's okay," she said. "I saw the manuscript was stacked differently after you left. When you had a look at the bed."

"I thought you were asleep," I said.

"Maybe I was pretending," she said. "Like the dead man."

"What?" my brother said.

"What did you think?" she said.

"I liked it. I liked the stories. The parrot one was good. The other two were scary. It didn't seem to be a memoir."

"Well, you know how it goes," she said.

I nodded, even though I didn't.

"Won't your agent be cross?" I said.

"He's too young. He's frightened of me," she said. "And besides, it's too good."

"I'm frightened of mine," I said.

"Good," my grandmother said, then she turned to my brother. "Where's your wife? Back at the house?"

"She went home," my brother said. "London, I mean."

"I understand," my grandmother said.

"It's nice to spend time. Just us."

"What were you boys fighting about?" she said.

"Sports," my brother said.

"Mum's manuscript," I said. "The video I told you about. What to do with the house."

"Have you asked your mother about it?"

"No," my brother said.

"I have," I said, "but she doesn't remember so well. She thinks it's a different book. From the one I read."

"Is it?" she said.

"I don't know."

"Have you read it?" our grandmother said, to my brother.

"Yeah," my brother said. "I mean, not really. I've seen what it is."

"And the video?" she said.

"It's just a video," my brother said.

"So you see different things in them," my grandmother said. "That's not something to fight about."

"It wasn't really about that," my brother said.

As we were leaving, our grandmother said she wanted to show me something.

"One moment, Gabriel," she said, "I want to show you something."

My brother was already out and getting in the car.

I followed my grandmother to the back of her house, where her windows looked out onto her back garden.

She got on her tiptoes and leaned on the kitchen counter. She peered at the garden.

"Look," she said. So I did.

In her garden was a deer-man.

He had the same muddy-brown costume as mine.

He had a trowel in his hand. He was on one knee. He was moving a potted plant I recognized as rosemary into the soil of her flowerbed, so it sat flanked by flowers that were potentially her last pansies before winter.

"Okay," I said.

"Do you understand?" my grandmother said.

"I don't know," I said.

"I know it's scary," she said, "but a garden is made of a million things. They help. When things need cutting down or new things need planting. You can't do it all on your own."

I looked out at everything.

"It is scary," I said.

"Yes," my grandmother said, smiling at me. "Of course it is."

Do you believe in parallel universes?" I said, to my brother. He was driving us back from our grandmother's house. The stereo was off now. The sun had come out a little. But mostly the sky was still cloudy.

"I don't know," my brother said. "I don't know enough about physics."

"I do," I said, "because you can imagine them."

We passed the field where my grandmother and I liked to look for deer. I looked for the deer. But there weren't any in there.

"It doesn't matter to me," my brother said. "I chose this one. This is the one I care about."

"Hm," I said.

My phone rang while I was out in the garden, smoking. It was night and I was alone. I recognized the number as my mother's care home. I picked up. I said hello.

"Hello?" I said.

My mother said it back.

"It's late," I told her.

"Yes," my mother said. "I wanted to call you. I remembered more about my manuscript. The one you were talking about. I remembered the end."

I exhaled. The smoke was visible from the light coming from the kitchen.

It went up to a place where it wasn't.

"Okay," I said.

"Guy's wife. She dies with the other man in the car. And Guy never knows why she was in the car."

"That's the beginning," I said, "not the end."

"Yes," my mother said. "You've read it."

"I think so."

"Then you remember the character at the beginning. Who Rebecca meets at the bus stop."

"Guy?" I said.

"No, that's Rebecca's husband. Rebecca meets another university professor while she is waiting at the bus stop. A nice lady called Professor Lovage. Rebecca tells her that she is going into town to buy polo shirts for Felix. He's starting school."

"I remember," I said.

"Years pass after Rebecca dies. Professor Lovage and Guy become very close, and eventually they fall in love. But Guy never knows why Rebecca was in the car, and where she was going with the other man."

"Yes," I said.

"And one night in the middle of summer, in the university botanical garden, they talk about the day Rebecca died for the first time. And Professor Lovage tells Guy that she met Rebecca the day she died. And that Rebecca was waiting for a bus to take her into town to buy polo shirts for Felix. Not having an affair with another man. Just waiting for a bus."

"But how does Guy know for sure?" I said.

"He doesn't," my mother said. "But he realizes that at some point you have to choose to just trust. And accept that you won't ever have all the answers."

"Right," I said.

"And that's how the book ends. But I don't remember if I wrote that down or not."

"All right, thanks, Mum," I said.

"I hope that's useful to you," she said.

"It is, Mum," I said. "I appreciate it."

And so, when my brother fell asleep in front of the television, I went upstairs to my mother's study to read the end of the manuscript.

Or whatever of it was there.

The pages of the manuscript were on the desk where I had left them, still slightly damp.

I was worried that there would be nothing there. Just title pages. Or that they had been damaged when my brother dropped them. Or that even if something was there, it would all be in the wrong order.

But flicking through the pages, the page numbers were in the right order. And the pages were full of words.

I didn't know how that was possible.

But it didn't seem to matter.

I thought about getting my brother, to show him. But I knew he wouldn't see it. So I didn't.

I just sat down and turned toward the end.

+

CHAPTER THIRTY-FOUR

Guy was driving too fast. It was night now. On long stretches of country road he would flick on the white Volvo's high beams so they could see farther into the forest.

"Slow down," Rebecca said.

"We don't have time," Guy said.

Rebecca gripped the armrest. She felt sure she'd see Felix run out in front of them. His small body breaking over the bonnet. Then at the side of the road, half his pale skin shed, one tiny arm broken behind his back.

"Please," she said.

"We don't have time," Guy said. "It's not much farther."

He accelerated.

Rebecca tried to force the image out of her head. Her eyes felt so wide.

She'd done what she'd promised. She looked across at him then back at the road. She put her hands together in her lap. Each felt colder than the other.

She felt herself shiver.

"I hope so," she said.

"I can barely see anything," Guy said.

He accelerated.

By the time they reached the tree, the moon had come out. It was almost full, or waning. Rebecca looked but did not see Felix. She just saw the black hedgerows and empty meadows and the lights of a single airplane against the sky.

And then Guy flicked on the high beams and Felix was there.

He slammed on the brakes.

Rebecca shouted.

But Felix was not in the road, broken over the car. He was lying, motionless, curled up in the folds of his winter coat, at the roots of the black tree that appeared at once alive and dead.

Rebecca looked for the pool of blood.

"Stop," she shouted again.

Rebecca opened the door before the car finished moving.

Felix was so still.

She went over to him.

Guy left the engine running and got out of the car too. Rebecca was with Felix now. She put one arm under his small head and moved his body so that he was facing upward, toward the sky. His skin was an almost transparent blue color, pale with the cold and the light from the car.

Rebecca shook him. She couldn't feel him breathing.

Then she saw the skin of Felix's forehead. The white ridge of dead skin across his brow, the pink-red scratch marks from tiny fingernails on the new skin underneath. Rebecca yelped. Then she breathed in. Then she put her head into Felix's tiny chest and made a sound from the bottom of her throat.

Guy was with her now. She left her face in Felix's chest. His winter coat was cold against her skin. She felt Guy's hand on her back. She smelled petrol. She heaved. Her chest contracted all the way in. Then she breathed out again.

She looked up slightly, through the branches of the possibly dying tree. The clouds were clearing fast. And she could see the far-away stars beating down on her softly, like summer rain through wind, from thousands of years back, and before her the possibly dying tree was dark and leafless and moving slowly against the blue-black sky.

And beneath her, Rebecca felt Felix move.

She looked down. She saw his face move. She made a noise from farther up in her throat.

"Felix," she said. "Felix."

Felix made a noise. He scrunched up his face.

"Mum?" he said.

"It's me, Felix, it's me."

"I can't see, Mum," he said.

And Rebecca saw that the transparent blue skin that covered his face was dead.

"It's all right," she said, "just listen to my voice. Don't move. Just listen to my voice."

Guy knelt down beside Felix and put his arms underneath him and picked him up slightly, supported his small head.

Rebecca put her thumbnails under the dead skin on Felix's forehead, softly, carefully avoiding the red-pink scratches on his new skin underneath.

"Just listen to my voice," she said. "It's all right."

And slowly, repeating that phrase, Rebecca lifted the blue and dead skin from Felix's face until it broke off at his chin.

And Felix twisted his eyes and opened his eyes for the first time, blinking up at her in the moonlight, and opened his mouth, and Rebecca saw his tiny teeth and his light brown eyes and she began to cry.

"You're here," he said. "You fixed it. I knew you'd be here."

That night as I was falling asleep, my girlfriend called me, too.

I picked up without even letting it ring a little bit.

"Hey," she said. There was no background noise behind her voice.

"Are you okay?" I said.

"Yeah. Are you?"

"I think so," I said.

"That's good," she said. She sounded sober.

"Why did you call?" I said.

"I just wanted to say that I'm sorry. For just leaving like that. With everything going on. I'm very sorry."

"I'm sorry, too," I said.

"I had to do it," she said. "That doesn't mean I wanted to."

"I know," I said.

"Sometimes you have to do things," she said.

"I know," I said, "it doesn't matter."

"It does matter," she said.

"Yeah," I said, "I know. But no more than anything else."

"A little more," she said.

"A little more," I said.

We were silent together. Then I decided to speak again.

"I do understand. You had to go. I was a mess. I was trying

to be so many things at once. All of me was trying to go in every direction. So I didn't have to choose. But you end up in pieces."

"Yeah," she said.

She was silent again for a moment.

Outside I could hear the motorway sound coming through the trees. There was no light left of the day.

I thought about the trillion cars, herds of headlights arching over hills. All pointing in the direction they were going. Night rain discovered the next morning. An airplane overhead.

Then she spoke again.

"It's growing up," she said. "You have to choose sometime. Then you have to live there."

Afterward I dressed and put on shoes.

I went outside.

I went to the bottom of the garden.

I took the padlock off the shed door. I left it slightly ajar.

Then I went back inside, and upstairs, and to bed, and was quickly pulled backward into my own eyelids.

The next morning my brother's wife came back to the house. We hugged. But we didn't say anything really.

My brother made us all coffee. We sat together at the breakfast bar.

I waited for my thoughts to become one thing. But they didn't. So I just started saying what I wanted to say.

"I'm sorry," I said. I looked at my brother's wife, then down.

"I'm sorry, too," my brother's wife said.

I shrugged. I looked at her again, then at my brother.

"We've been talking," my brother's wife said.

"Six months," my brother said, "we can get by. Without selling."

"Are you sure?" I said.

"If Dad hadn't died we would have had to, anyway."

"We can think about it again in the spring," my brother's wife said.

"You're sure," I said.

"We are," my brother said. "Just look after it all properly."

"Okay," I said, "thank you."

"Thank you for sorting the creeper, by the way," my brother's wife said. "It looks much better."

"What?"

"The front garden. The Virginia creeper. The Russian vines. They were growing up the front of the house. Thank you for doing that."

"Oh," I said, "right."

We picked up my mother from the nursing home in the small and expensive car. My mother sat up front.

She was carrying my father in the blue and white vase, all of him combusted.

We were driving to some cliffs, which overlooked some sea. It was where my father had grown up, supposedly. But I didn't know how much time he'd spent just hanging out on the edge of cliffs.

We stopped at a services. My brother's wife helped my mother walk to the bathrooms. I stayed by the car with my brother, leaning on it.

I lit a cigarette.

"Can I have one of those?" my brother said. I threw the pack at him. He caught it, annoyingly.

I finished the cigarette and then took the vase with Dad in it from the front seat of the car.

"What are you doing?" my brother said.

"Dad didn't like cliffs," I said. "Dad liked service stations."

My brother made a strange face. Then he made a normal one.

"Okay," he said. "Don't take much. Leave enough for Mum."

We both took a handful of Dad-ash from the surprisingly large amount in the vase.

We put some on the steps of the service station.

We put some in front of the Starbucks refrigerator where they kept the juices and breakfast pots and sandwiches.

We put some in front of the counter at the Burger King, and some on the newspapers and magazines at the Waitrose.

Then we washed our hands and walked back to the car.

I lit another cigarette. I handed the pack to my brother. He lit one, too. We stood there in silence for a moment.

"That was the right thing to do," my brother said.

"Yeah," I said.

"I'm not talking to you. I'm talking to me."

"Okay," I said.

"Listen," my brother said. "It's good you believe things so sincerely. The estate agent. The house. All that. You think you don't believe in things, but you do."

"I do think I do," I said.

"Well, whatever. I know it gets you into trouble. But it's better to be like that than like me. It just makes it harder."

"Makes what harder?" I said. He gestured around, then at the car.

"All this," he said. "Building the thing that's real to you."

I didn't say anything. My mother and my brother's wife were walking back toward the car now.

I dropped my cigarette on the ground.

The wind was cold.

The long autumn shadow of the pine trees.

At the cliffs, our mother cried as she emptied the vase over the edge into the sea. I could feel the skin on my neck drying out and dying. I picked at it slightly. I wanted to ask what she would do with the vase, once Dad was all out of it. Would she keep it? Rinse it? Use it for flowers, or leave it empty?

In the bathroom, hours later, I picked at the skin on my neck. It pulled upward, up my chin, then the skin from my face started coming off. I just kept pulling, up my cheeks, around my nostrils, around my eyes and from my eyelids, up my forehead, right up to my hairline, where it tore off neatly, until I had a mask made from my own skin in my hands.

When everyone was gone, and I had the house to myself again, I went to see a good doctor, a reputable doctor, who you had to pay for.

"Yes," she said, "I can see what you mean."

"You can?" I said.

"There's a lot of bruising around your cheekbone. What did you say you did?"

"That's not why I'm here," I said.

"Why are you here?"

"All my skin is peeling off."

"That sounds like eczema," she said.

"No, it's not eczema. It comes off in huge sheets. My whole chest came off. My whole face came off. Like a reptile."

She tilted her head and looked at me for a moment.

"And what's under the skin?"

"What?"

"What's underneath? When the skin comes off. Does it bleed?"

"No," I said, "it's just more skin."

"So what's the problem?"

"Excuse me?"

"If it's just the same skin underneath. What's the problem?"

I told her that I didn't know.

"Well. It probably feels very dramatic," she said, "but I wouldn't worry so much."

"Okay," I said.

"I'm going to prescribe you a cream," she said, and started typing on her computer.

"Hydrocortisol?"

"Cortisone," she said. "There's a pharmacist next door, and you can pay the receptionist on your way out."

"All right," I said. I stood to leave. "Thank you for your time."

That night I dreamed I was in a New York hotel, stories above all of Manhattan. Out of the hotel windows I could see the whole sky and its lights.

My mother was there. So was my brother. We were in the living room of a suite, waiting for something. There was a sliding door to the hotel bedroom.

We were all so happy, my brother and my mother and me, talking and laughing about things that had happened to us that we all remembered. To pass the time while we waited.

And at some point, while we were laughing, the sliding door to the bedroom opened. And I saw my father there.

But not quite my father. The younger, trimmer, cleaner version of my father.

My child version of him, that I'd kind of forgotten about.

He looked so sheepish and confident and handsome. He didn't look at me. He was looking out of the window, at all of his lights, like time-stuck falling stars, lighting his rolled-up cigarette.

And my brother said: "Guess it's my turn." And my brother went into the bedroom where our father was waiting for him.

And the sliding door closed and that was the last I saw of them both.

And I knew that Dad was telling my brother something really important in there. And that it was my turn to hear the important thing next.

And right then I realized that it was a dream.

And I was desperate to see Dad, and talk to him, and hear the important thing.

And I tried so hard to stay in the dream.

I tried and tried and tried.

I wanted to see Dad so much.

I tried so hard.

But my eyes opened.

And my brother was gone.

And my mother was gone.

And Dad was gone, completely.

And here it was sunshine and day.

I dressed and went downstairs. I felt hungry. But in a good way. I couldn't remember when the last time I'd eaten was. But it didn't seem to matter.

I looked in the fridge.

The fridge was full of groceries from supermarket time.

I took butter from the fridge and I took eggs.

I took beautiful red and yellow tomatoes. Basil that smelled pepper sweet. Rosemary.

I washed it all down with coffee and sparkling water from a cold and blue can.

Then I sat there for a bit and thought about my dad.

Then I decided to get to work.

So I took my laptop into my mother's study and deleted all the emails from my agent.

Then I went into my bank account and sent almost all of the book money to my brother, with a note saying: "rent."

Then I went downstairs into my father's study. I collected as many of his papers as I could carry and took them all up to my mother's study.

Then I collected all my favorite house books from their shelves and boxes and took them up to my mother's study, too.

Then I set all of the papers and books down on my mother's desk and opened my mother's manuscript at the first page so that I could copy from that and my father's papers and all my favorite house books easily.

Then I began to type:

I was in the waiting room. Then I was in the examination room.

Acknowledgments

I received an overwhelming amount of kindness and support whilst working on this novel. I am so grateful it hurts.

But I want to particularly thank my mother, Rebecca Smith, my father, Stephen Smith, my grandmother, Shena Mackay, my first real girlfriend, Jacquetta Bridge, my aunt, Cecily Brown, and my best friend, Greg Probert.

This novel would not exist without Giancarlo DiTrapano, who edited it and was going to publish it before he passed in 2021. I miss you every day. I hope I have made you proud.

Nor would it exist without Jordan Castro, Emma Adler, Rebecca Panovka, Kiara Barrow, Kristi Murray, Jackie Ko, and Chris White.

Thanks also to Tracy Bohan, Rebecca O'Connor, Will Govan, Mr. Savvas, Lucretia Stewart, Adam Hyslop, Darius Bradbury, Clancy Martin, Tadanari Lee, Gordon Lish, Piers Blofeld, Holly Crook, Bruce and Sarah Clark, Ian Van Wye, Robin Brown, and Mark, Jan, and Tom Probert.

I'm so grateful to all my friends, but particularly Lily Hackett, Catherine Foulkrod, Sam Hurst, Ed Stennett, Isobel McGrigor, Rob Thompson, Dominic Fenton, George

Barsoum, Matthew Claydon, Andrew Dellar, Paul Johnathan, Maria Gouverneur McKeown.

Also to Gian's husband, Guiseppe Avallone, and the Giancarlo DiTrapano Foundation, who are doing wonderful, wonderful work.

And Sarah Salmean—forever, and always.

A NOTE ON THE TYPE

The body text of this book was set in Janson Pro. It is part of a set of old-style serif typefaces from the Dutch Baroque period, and modern revivals from the twentieth century. Janson is a crisp serif, and relatively high-contrast in its design, most popular for body text. It was named after Anton Janson (1620–1687), a Leipzig-based printer and punch cutter from the Netherlands who was believed to have created them. In 1954, however, an essay was published asserting that the designer of the typeface was in fact a Hungarian-Transylvanian schoolmaster and punch cutter, Miklós (Nicholas) Tótfalusi Kis (1650–1702).